JUST RIGHT

(A Cami Lark Mystery —Book Three)

BLAKE PIERCE

Blake Pierce

Blake Pierce is the USA Today bestselling author of the RILEY PAGE mystery series, which includes seventeen books. Blake Pierce is also the author of the MACKENZIE WHITE mystery series, comprising fourteen books; of the AVERY BLACK mystery series, comprising six books; of the KERI LOCKE mystery series, comprising five books; of the MAKING OF RILEY PAIGE mystery series, comprising six books; of the KATE WISE mystery series, comprising seven books; of the CHLOE FINE psychological suspense mystery, comprising six books; of the JESSIE HUNT psychological suspense thriller series, comprising twenty six books; of the AU PAIR psychological suspense thriller series, comprising three books; of the ZOE PRIME mystery series, comprising six books; of the ADELE SHARP mystery series, comprising sixteen books, of the EUROPEAN VOYAGE cozy mystery series, comprising six books; of the LAURA FROST FBI suspense thriller, comprising eleven books; of the ELLA DARK FBI suspense thriller, comprising fourteen books (and counting); of the A YEAR IN EUROPE cozy mystery series, comprising nine books, of the AVA GOLD mystery series, comprising six books (and counting); of the RACHEL GIFT mystery series, comprising ten books (and counting); of the VALERIE LAW mystery series, comprising nine books (and counting); of the PAIGE KING mystery series, comprising eight books (and counting); of the MAY MOORE mystery series, comprising eleven books (and counting); the CORA SHIELDS mystery series, comprising five books (and counting); of the NICKY LYONS mystery series, comprising seven books (and counting), of the CAMI LARK mystery series, comprising five books (and counting), and of the new AMBER YOUNG mystery series, comprising five books (and counting).

An avid reader and lifelong fan of the mystery and thriller genres, Blake loves to hear from you, so please feel free to visit www.blakepierceauthor.com to learn more and stay in touch.

ISBN: 978-1-0943-3035-8

BOOKS BY BLAKE PIERCE

AMBER YOUNG MYSTERY SERIES
ABSENT PITY (Book #1)
ABSENT REMORSE (Book #2)
ABSENT FEELING (Book #3)
ABSENT MERCY (Book #4)
ABSENT REASON (Book #5)

CAMI LARK MYSTERY SERIES
JUST ME (Book #1)
JUST OUTSIDE (Book #2)
JUST RIGHT (Book #3)
JUST FORGET (Book #4)
JUST ONCE (Book #5)

NICKY LYONS MYSTERY SERIES
ALL MINE (Book #1)
ALL HIS (Book #2)
ALL HE SEES (Book #3)
ALL ALONE (Book #4)
ALL FOR ONE (Book #5)
ALL HE TAKES (Book #6)
ALL FOR ME (Book #7)

CORA SHIELDS MYSTERY SERIES
UNDONE (Book #1)
UNWANTED (Book #2)
UNHINGED (Book #3)
UNSAID (Book #4)
UNGLUED (Book #5)

MAY MOORE SUSPENSE THRILLER
NEVER RUN (Book #1)
NEVER TELL (Book #2)
NEVER LIVE (Book #3)
NEVER HIDE (Book #4)
NEVER FORGIVE (Book #5)
NEVER AGAIN (Book #6)

NEVER LOOK BACK (Book #7)
NEVER FORGET (Book #8)
NEVER LET GO (Book #9)
NEVER PRETEND (Book #10)
NEVER HESITATE (Book #11)

PAIGE KING MYSTERY SERIES
THE GIRL HE PINED (Book #1)
THE GIRL HE CHOSE (Book #2)
THE GIRL HE TOOK (Book #3)
THE GIRL HE WISHED (Book #4)
THE GIRL HE CROWNED (Book #5)
THE GIRL HE WATCHED (Book #6)
THE GIRL HE WANTED (Book #7)
THE GIRL HE CLAIMED (Book #8)

VALERIE LAW MYSTERY SERIES
NO MERCY (Book #1)
NO PITY (Book #2)
NO FEAR (Book #3)
NO SLEEP (Book #4)
NO QUARTER (Book #5)
NO CHANCE (Book #6)
NO REFUGE (Book #7)
NO GRACE (Book #8)
NO ESCAPE (Book #9)

RACHEL GIFT MYSTERY SERIES
HER LAST WISH (Book #1)
HER LAST CHANCE (Book #2)
HER LAST HOPE (Book #3)
HER LAST FEAR (Book #4)
HER LAST CHOICE (Book #5)
HER LAST BREATH (Book #6)
HER LAST MISTAKE (Book #7)
HER LAST DESIRE (Book #8)
HER LAST REGRET (Book #9)
HER LAST HOUR (Book #10)

AVA GOLD MYSTERY SERIES
CITY OF PREY (Book #1)

CITY OF FEAR (Book #2)
CITY OF BONES (Book #3)
CITY OF GHOSTS (Book #4)
CITY OF DEATH (Book #5)
CITY OF VICE (Book #6)

A YEAR IN EUROPE
A MURDER IN PARIS (Book #1)
DEATH IN FLORENCE (Book #2)
VENGEANCE IN VIENNA (Book #3)
A FATALITY IN SPAIN (Book #4)

ELLA DARK FBI SUSPENSE THRILLER
GIRL, ALONE (Book #1)
GIRL, TAKEN (Book #2)
GIRL, HUNTED (Book #3)
GIRL, SILENCED (Book #4)
GIRL, VANISHED (Book 5)
GIRL ERASED (Book #6)
GIRL, FORSAKEN (Book #7)
GIRL, TRAPPED (Book #8)
GIRL, EXPENDABLE (Book #9)
GIRL, ESCAPED (Book #10)
GIRL, HIS (Book #11)
GIRL, LURED (Book #12)
GIRL, MISSING (Book #13)
GIRL, UNKNOWN (Book #14)

LAURA FROST FBI SUSPENSE THRILLER
ALREADY GONE (Book #1)
ALREADY SEEN (Book #2)
ALREADY TRAPPED (Book #3)
ALREADY MISSING (Book #4)
ALREADY DEAD (Book #5)
ALREADY TAKEN (Book #6)
ALREADY CHOSEN (Book #7)
ALREADY LOST (Book #8)
ALREADY HIS (Book #9)
ALREADY LURED (Book #10)
ALREADY COLD (Book #11)

EUROPEAN VOYAGE COZY MYSTERY SERIES

MURDER (AND BAKLAVA) (Book #1)
DEATH (AND APPLE STRUDEL) (Book #2)
CRIME (AND LAGER) (Book #3)
MISFORTUNE (AND GOUDA) (Book #4)
CALAMITY (AND A DANISH) (Book #5)
MAYHEM (AND HERRING) (Book #6)

ADELE SHARP MYSTERY SERIES

LEFT TO DIE (Book #1)
LEFT TO RUN (Book #2)
LEFT TO HIDE (Book #3)
LEFT TO KILL (Book #4)
LEFT TO MURDER (Book #5)
LEFT TO ENVY (Book #6)
LEFT TO LAPSE (Book #7)
LEFT TO VANISH (Book #8)
LEFT TO HUNT (Book #9)
LEFT TO FEAR (Book #10)
LEFT TO PREY (Book #11)
LEFT TO LURE (Book #12)
LEFT TO CRAVE (Book #13)
LEFT TO LOATHE (Book #14)
LEFT TO HARM (Book #15)
LEFT TO RUIN (Book #16)

THE AU PAIR SERIES

ALMOST GONE (Book#1)
ALMOST LOST (Book #2)
ALMOST DEAD (Book #3)

ZOE PRIME MYSTERY SERIES

FACE OF DEATH (Book#1)
FACE OF MURDER (Book #2)
FACE OF FEAR (Book #3)
FACE OF MADNESS (Book #4)
FACE OF FURY (Book #5)
FACE OF DARKNESS (Book #6)

A JESSIE HUNT PSYCHOLOGICAL SUSPENSE SERIES

THE PERFECT WIFE (Book #1)

THE PERFECT BLOCK (Book #2)
THE PERFECT HOUSE (Book #3)
THE PERFECT SMILE (Book #4)
THE PERFECT LIE (Book #5)
THE PERFECT LOOK (Book #6)
THE PERFECT AFFAIR (Book #7)
THE PERFECT ALIBI (Book #8)
THE PERFECT NEIGHBOR (Book #9)
THE PERFECT DISGUISE (Book #10)
THE PERFECT SECRET (Book #11)
THE PERFECT FAÇADE (Book #12)
THE PERFECT IMPRESSION (Book #13)
THE PERFECT DECEIT (Book #14)
THE PERFECT MISTRESS (Book #15)
THE PERFECT IMAGE (Book #16)
THE PERFECT VEIL (Book #17)
THE PERFECT INDISCRETION (Book #18)
THE PERFECT RUMOR (Book #19)
THE PERFECT COUPLE (Book #20)
THE PERFECT MURDER (Book #21)
THE PERFECT HUSBAND (Book #22)
THE PERFECT SCANDAL (Book #23)
THE PERFECT MASK (Book #24)
THE PERFECT RUSE (Book #25)
THE PERFECT VENEER (Book #26)

CHLOE FINE PSYCHOLOGICAL SUSPENSE SERIES

NEXT DOOR (Book #1)
A NEIGHBOR'S LIE (Book #2)
CUL DE SAC (Book #3)
SILENT NEIGHBOR (Book #4)
HOMECOMING (Book #5)
TINTED WINDOWS (Book #6)

KATE WISE MYSTERY SERIES

IF SHE KNEW (Book #1)
IF SHE SAW (Book #2)
IF SHE RAN (Book #3)
IF SHE HID (Book #4)
IF SHE FLED (Book #5)
IF SHE FEARED (Book #6)

IF SHE HEARD (Book #7)

THE MAKING OF RILEY PAIGE SERIES
WATCHING (Book #1)
WAITING (Book #2)
LURING (Book #3)
TAKING (Book #4)
STALKING (Book #5)
KILLING (Book #6)

RILEY PAIGE MYSTERY SERIES
ONCE GONE (Book #1)
ONCE TAKEN (Book #2)
ONCE CRAVED (Book #3)
ONCE LURED (Book #4)
ONCE HUNTED (Book #5)
ONCE PINED (Book #6)
ONCE FORSAKEN (Book #7)
ONCE COLD (Book #8)
ONCE STALKED (Book #9)
ONCE LOST (Book #10)
ONCE BURIED (Book #11)
ONCE BOUND (Book #12)
ONCE TRAPPED (Book #13)
ONCE DORMANT (Book #14)
ONCE SHUNNED (Book #15)
ONCE MISSED (Book #16)
ONCE CHOSEN (Book #17)

MACKENZIE WHITE MYSTERY SERIES
BEFORE HE KILLS (Book #1)
BEFORE HE SEES (Book #2)
BEFORE HE COVETS (Book #3)
BEFORE HE TAKES (Book #4)
BEFORE HE NEEDS (Book #5)
BEFORE HE FEELS (Book #6)
BEFORE HE SINS (Book #7)
BEFORE HE HUNTS (Book #8)
BEFORE HE PREYS (Book #9)
BEFORE HE LONGS (Book #10)
BEFORE HE LAPSES (Book #11)

BEFORE HE ENVIES (Book #12)
BEFORE HE STALKS (Book #13)
BEFORE HE HARMS (Book #14)

AVERY BLACK MYSTERY SERIES
CAUSE TO KILL (Book #1)
CAUSE TO RUN (Book #2)
CAUSE TO HIDE (Book #3)
CAUSE TO FEAR (Book #4)
CAUSE TO SAVE (Book #5)
CAUSE TO DREAD (Book #6)

KERI LOCKE MYSTERY SERIES
A TRACE OF DEATH (Book #1)
A TRACE OF MURDER (Book #2)
A TRACE OF VICE (Book #3)
A TRACE OF CRIME (Book #4)
A TRACE OF HOPE (Book #5)

PROLOGUE

The waters of the dolphin pool were still, the seating surrounding it bare and empty, and Patti Browne let out a silent curse as she strode into the enclosure. Never mind missing the show, she wasn't even in time for the interaction and feeding afterward. She'd been delayed getting out of town. Her meetings had run late, traffic had been diabolical, and now this event, and the chance for all the photos, were gone.

She stared around her, letting out an angry sigh as she considered her limited options. Or maybe they weren't that limited. It felt as if two people were warring inside her.

The first, her mother's calm voice, was saying, "Go home, Patti. You're late, and it's your fault. Be a nice human being, respect the aquarium's rules, and don't cause problems."

The second, her own strident voice, was giving different advice, "Patti, you need to stand up for yourself. Remember, the customer is always right, especially in these days of phones and social media. You're a high-profile individual with a large following. They must give you an experience, even though you're too late for the show. Don't you let them treat you like dirt! You're not a doormat like your mother!"

She hadn't gotten to where she was, with a successful career as a special effects make-up artist, by being someone who never stood up for herself. She pushed the boundaries; she was that woman who called the manager, who demanded a free ticket because she didn't get a good seat, who would march into the aquarium even though the show was over and tell them that she was here and that they should do something about it.

The problem was that she didn't see anyone around.

Was it really too late? Or were the dolphins still eating? They were not in the pool, but they must be in their state-of-the-art glass-fronted aquarium where they returned to after the performance.

That must be beyond the pool somewhere.

Patti shivered, feeling the evening breeze cool and sharp. Without the music and the hordes of spectators, without the sunshine and the lights, this place felt strangely bleak and surprisingly creepy. The waters of the pool were dark, and it was silent. Not a soul around. It was very different from when the public was here, and it was filled with activity.

Now, with a chill wind blowing through the seats, flapping the flags and bunting that only she was there to see, it felt a lot less friendly.

She knew she probably should not have sneaked through the unmanned turnstile and past the notice saying “Closed,” but she'd thought she would be in time, at least, to see the end of it and get those all-important photos that her followers were now waiting for.

Where was the main aquarium? Perhaps there were a few people still there. If she remembered from the last time she'd been here, which was years ago, you could go down the lower passageway that led to the glass tanks. Or you could go up the stairs that led to the tank area itself.

Hesitant now, because this was feeling a lot like trespassing, she walked around the pool to where she thought she remembered the doors were.

"Hello?" she called. "Is anyone there? Am I in time for the feeding? Is there any chance of getting some service here?"

Patti walked around the pool, peering down the dark passages that led into the building, wondering where they ended up. There were no signs pointing her in the direction of the tanks; no way of finding out. Now, she thought she’d misremembered, or maybe they’d changed the layout. It had been ages since she’d last been here. She couldn’t see signage anywhere, so maybe the layout had been changed.

Feeling more and more like an intruder, Patti started to walk to the stairs she saw ahead. Perhaps they would lead to the upper viewing deck. Was this the right way, up these narrow, metal steps?

She was feeling very uneasy. It was too quiet here. She should turn back and head out.

But her own determination to have things her way wouldn't let her do that. She was here now, and she was so close to the dolphin tank. It was ridiculous not to be able to view them, especially since she'd already posted online that photos were coming this evening.

The dolphins weren't going to disappear after the show was over. They were still around somewhere and would probably love a photo op with a latecomer.

She was sure she would find the way to the main aquarium if she went up here. Or else, find someone who could help. If she asked nicely, perhaps they would feed one fish to them while she watched. Just one. Her footsteps clanged on the steel.

And then, from behind her, from the other side of the pool, she heard the quick thudding of footsteps and a man's voice shout, "Hey there!"

She paused, letting go of the stair rail, turning to see who was approaching her.

She couldn't see clearly enough. From this higher angle, the lights in the parking lot next door were shining into her eyes, and he was nothing more than a dark silhouette. But the brisk, purposeful way he was heading toward her clued her in that he was an employee and that she was somewhere she shouldn't be.

"Hi, I got here late. I'm hoping I can see the dolphins still. Do you know if that's possible?" she asked, hearing the familiar mix of politeness and authority in her own voice that she was sure would get her the results she expected.

But he didn't respond, and there was something about the way he was approaching her, something aggressive in his stance, that was making her nervous.

"Gail," he said, his voice hoarse. "Gail!"

"I'm not Gail," she replied, trying for the disdainful topspin in her tone that usually put an end to trouble.

"Gail," he said again, and began walking even faster toward her.

Now, the veneer of denial she'd had, with her own self-righteous attitude, shattered.

This was trouble. It was bad trouble. And suddenly, apart from this man, now half-running toward her, she realized how alone she was here.

Patti turned and ran up the staircase, her feet clattering on the metal treads. She was going as fast as she could, but he was gaining on her, his footsteps pounding behind her.

"Gail," he said, his voice hoarse and rough. "Come back! You know you don't have to run away. Is it you, Gail? Is it really you?"

Something about the way he said it made her feel a rising sense of horror. She shouldn't be here. She shouldn't have sneaked in. And now she was trapped in these deserted premises, with a strange man who sounded as though he was out of breath, but who was also running scarily fast up the stairs behind her.

She reached the top of the stairs, but there was nowhere to go. Nowhere! She was on a small viewing deck overlooking the pool. It felt like a trap. Her breath was heaving in her chest.

He advanced on her, looming.

"No, don't do this, you'll regret it, you mustn't, you can't! Not now, not me! Please!" The words spilled out of her in a terrified babble.

"Oh, Gail," he hissed. “Oh, no!”

She felt something hit her head hard, so hard her vision exploded, and she blacked out instantly.

She never felt herself topple over the edge of the rail, her unconscious form freefalling down, to land with a splash in the dark waters of the pool below.

From above, the killer watched her sink.

Breathing hard, he waited, watching the waves turn to ripples, and then to the merest shimmer of dark reflected light, like negative space around the object in the pool, now unmoving and lifeless.

It was done.

But he knew, deep inside, that it wasn't over.

CHAPTER ONE

Was she going to do it?

Cami Lark had been agonizing over her decision for most of the night. She'd been sitting in her student digs at MIT, holed up in the tiny bedroom, messaging her friend on the dark web as she tried to build up the resolve, the courage, and the sheer bloody mindedness to do what she longed to do.

That was to sneak back into the FBI archives and try again to pull the information on her sister Jenna's missing persons file.

Last time she'd tried, the file had corrupted thanks to malware embedded in the record archive. Worse still, there had been a tracking program tacked onto the file which she hadn't seen in time, and Cami knew that someone might know who she was. Someone in the FBI might already be aware that she was trying to open this mysteriously corrupted file to find out exactly what had happened to her older sister Jenna, who had disappeared when Cami was just fifteen years old.

The FBI had investigated, but nothing had ever come of it. Cami had always wondered why. Recently, she'd been co-opted into the FBI to help with cases that required IT expertise, and she'd thought it was her chance to find out. But she knew she was on dangerous ground, especially since the reason she'd been co-opted in the first place was as an alternative to going to prison after the FBI had caught her hacking their main website homepage.

So, she knew that there was a strong chance this foray could end in disaster. But still, she had to try.

This time, Cami's friend had shown her some open source coding that she thought might help her get around the problem. Cami had tweaked the coding, and she thought it was a workable solution. All she needed now was the courage.

"Done it yet?" It was her friend, Amo-1, messaging again.

"Not yet." Cami drained what must have been her sixth cup of black coffee that night. She turned to the energy drink on the desk, cracked it open, and downed that as well. The faintest chirps of birdsong were filtering in through the still dark windows. The time was four-thirty

a.m. Her eyes felt reddened, her body felt tired, but her mind felt sharp, like a knife.

"What you waiting for?"

"I don't know."

Almost of their own volition, Cami watched her fingers move over the keyboard. She'd painted her fingernails black to match the color of her dyed hair, with its daring, partly shaven style, and the color of the dark tattoos on her arms.

"Won't wait forever. Do it or don't do it. Whatever it is???"

She hadn't told Amo-1, her anonymous but trusted friend, exactly what her covert mission involved. Cami knew that if anyone found out—anyone other than whoever had inserted the tracking program earlier—she'd be in huge trouble. It could destroy the uneasy relationship she currently had with the FBI. After all, the fact that they'd said they would drop the charges against her if she was willing to help with IT-related cases, didn't mean they couldn't reinstate them again. Cami didn't fully trust the FBI. Even though she now admitted to herself that there were good people working there, there were also people like the one who'd embedded this malware into the case archive.

Now, biting her lip, she agonized once more over her decision.

It surely wasn't wrong to go in and see the file. Especially since she'd never been able to work out why the case had been so neglected, almost as if it had been hushed up. Combined with the malware, Cami was wondering if there were criminal forces at work within the FBI itself. This wasn't regular policy, that was for sure. This was highly irregular.

If she did this—and was able to find out who'd tampered with the file—she might actually be helping the FBI.

But she'd also be putting herself in danger. She had no illusions about that at all. This was not going to go well for her if whoever had taken all these precautions to hide the information caught up with her.

"I'm scared," she typed.

"Fears must be faced," Amo-1 typed.

"Do or die?" Cami retorted with a skull emoji.

"If you don't do it now, I got to go."

"I'm doing it."

Her fingers were trembling. She could feel her breath coming fast and shallow. Her heart was pounding. But she was not leaving this alone. They were not doing this to her. Whoever this person was, she was not going to let them win.

Taking a deep breath, her fingers flew over the keys. Speed was of the essence here, and it could save her skin.

"You are accessing classified information. To continue, please enter your password."

That was the same warning she'd gotten last time.

Cami typed in her password. It wasn't one she had needed to hack. It was a standard access password that she'd used on the first case she'd handled. The archives were not as highly classified as the main FBI database, and it seemed that these passwords weren't changed as often.

She was ready with a work-around if she needed it, but the password got her in. And then, she delved deeply into the history, looking for the file she needed.

There it was. Jenna Lark, followed by a number. The same file, with the same malware loaded that had made it unreadable. But this time, she had an ally on her side. A clever program, written by some anonymous hacker with a stratospheric IQ. Shared on open source, it had been found by her friend and then sent to Cami, who had looked at the code and added her own adjustments to the program based on what she knew of the damaged file.

Now, it was do or die time.

She watched as the file downloaded.

It didn't seem to take long. Cami stared at it on her screen, her heart pounding in her chest. There were no warnings now. This was good. This was progress.

For approximately the thousandth time that night, she wondered if she was doing the right thing. That was a question she couldn't answer. Because she might not know until trouble landed.

"Well, are you doing it?" Amo-1 messaged impatiently.

"Yes," Cami said out loud, to herself. "Yes, I'm doing it."

She felt sick with nerves. Her stomach felt like it was full of lead.

"Done it?" Amo-1 messaged.

"I'm busy with it." Cami gritted her teeth. She felt exposed here. She felt as if, somewhere, alarm bells were sounding and unfriendly eyes were turning her way, observing what she was doing, already working to track her presence there.

She thought if she had been a real spy, it would be a lot easier. It might be exciting, not terrifying. But then, she wasn't a real spy. She wasn't even a real FBI agent. She was a student hacker who'd been roped in when she'd been arrested. It had been a choice between a clean slate, if she accepted the FBI's offer, or to go to prison for twenty years, if she didn’t accept their offer.

"I really have to get going," Amo-1 typed. *"Did it work?"*

Cami's fingers flew, her nerves singing like violin strings. She was aware of how quickly time was passing. Outside her window, it was getting lighter.

She downloaded the file. It looked identical to the one before.

"It's accessed," she typed.

Amo-1 responded with a fist pump and a fingers crossed.

Her throat was dry as dust. Her heart was pounding. She felt sick.

But she was almost there. There was no time to check the file because now, she needed to get out and get away before anyone could grasp onto the trace of her presence due to this illicit foray into the records.

Out and away. It had to be done perfectly. Flawlessly, and cold-mindedly. No room for panic. Every step had to be backtracked and erased, and all the while, she had to keep an eye out for anyone who might be deploying software to track her or leaving a trap.

Cami didn't think that this was something she should have to worry about when exiting archives. The fact that she had to indicated a malevolent presence. An enemy within the organization.

But there was no time to think about that. Everything needed to be in place. Erase, repeat, reverse.

And finally, with a huge sigh, she was out. Her hands were shaking. She felt like she'd just run a hundred-yard dash. But the file was now on her desktop.

Same file. It looked the same. It had taken less time to download, and she didn't yet know if that was good or bad.

Now, she had to find out if it worked and if she could access the contents and the information within.

"Opening it," she typed.

Holding her breath, Cami double-clicked the folder and waited to see what appeared.

CHAPTER TWO

Cami felt breathless. She felt as if she'd been on an actual physical raid into the archives. But where a physical raid would tell her instantly if she'd been seen, she knew that it wouldn't be as easy to tell if she'd gotten away free and clear now.

Only time would show her that. But in the meantime, she could see what she had.

The folder opened, and she let out a long, shaky breath.

It had worked! The program to counter the malware had done its job, and Cami sent a silent thank you and good vibes to the faceless, unknown genius who'd hunched over his or her keyboard, figuring out the coding necessary to counter the program that had—virtually—shredded the file as it had been extracted.

At times like this, she felt a flare of happiness and pride that she was connected to this weird, intangible network of genius and ideas. People thought of hackers as bad, but there were only a few who used their powers to harm. Many more used them to solve problems, to fix issues, and to progress technology. They were channeled for good, rather than bad.

"It's not damaged," she messaged to Amo-1.

"Brilliant!" A flood of happy emojis followed, and then a quick, *"Chat later!"*

"Thank you," Cami typed back.

Amo-1 signed off, and Cami eagerly turned her attention to the copy of the file.

She was startled to see how meager it was. Having had some limited experience of cases in the FBI so far, she was used to what they contained. And by comparison, this didn't have much.

"So, what's here?" she muttered to herself.

There was the missing persons report to say when and where Jenna Lark had last been seen, with a description of her sister and an attached photo. That was correct, even though those stark black and white words bore no relation to the emotions Cami had felt.

The confusion and heartache had filled her world. This had been her big sister, her rock. Her protector from the harsh authority of her father's rule, where even her mother tiptoed around him, meek and submissive.

In that household, there hadn't been much love to be found, and a large part of what there had been had come from Jenna. When she'd disappeared, it felt as if Cami's world had shattered. The pain had never gone away, and she felt it now as she looked at the photo in the case file—Jenna, her pale blonde hair short and spiky, that cheeky smile on her face.

They had done some work, Cami saw. They'd interviewed a few neighbors, trying to find out if Jenna had been seen, or if she'd said anything to give a hint as to where she might have gone. But there was no clue, no lead. No real information in that sparse file, and it made her wonder if something was completely missing from it or had been physically taken out.

Her heart felt leaden. She had always hoped, all these years, that Jenna was still alive. It was all that had kept her going. The knowledge, however fragile and uncertain, that the sister she'd loved so much was still out there. Living her life, waiting to come home. Or perhaps she was in darker circumstances, kept prisoner, or held by someone and coerced into staying away from her family for some unknown reason. Cami's imagination had always run ahead with scenarios.

But perhaps she had been deceiving herself all this time. Perhaps Jenna was dead, and she had been clinging to a fake dream. It could be that there was nothing to be found, and she'd have to accept that. People went missing. Runaways got murdered. Accidents happened. Of course, it was the not knowing that was the worst. Hadn’t the FBI cared about that?

Who had investigated this file, anyway? Cami wondered with a sudden rush of anger. *Who'd done such a half-assed job on it?*

She looked for the investigating agent's name. Liam Treverton. That was who had been in charge. Agent Treverton.

Cami frowned, feeling unsure as she wondered if Treverton had been the one to plant the malware.

Did he know what she'd done? Where was he, and how was he connected with the FBI? It could be disastrous for her if he was still working in the Boston office. Suddenly curious, and concerned, she turned to her keyboard and looked up his name.

Now, this was interesting. Her eyes widened as she read it. Just a couple of years ago, Agent Treverton had left the FBI.

"Why's that?" Cami muttered to herself, picking up her coffee cup yet again in the hope that one more caffeine-rich drop might remain if she tipped it all the way back. "Did he just leave? Or was there a reason?"

She was not going to give up on this. She went searching deeper. Trawling the buried information, she started looking into why he left. After a few minutes of intensive searching, she found a record online, partially hidden but still accessible to a determined searcher.

And there was her answer. He'd been fired. For "conduct unbecoming."

Fired! Cami hissed in a breath. The agent responsible for her sister's case had since been fired. Who was this guy? *Where* was he? She felt like she wanted to arrive on his doorstep and demand answers.

She looked up his address and saw that he still lived in Massachusetts, in a smaller town about an hour's drive outside of Boston.

Tapping her fingers on the desk, Cami thought about this. Theoretically, she could arrive on his doorstep. She could demand to know what had happened. Of course, he might not tell her. What would she do then? There might be things she could do.

Staring at his ID photo with active hatred, Cami thought his face reflected his personality. He had cold blue eyes, a hard jaw, and an uncompromising expression. He had a cruel face, she decided. She wouldn't have wanted him looking into her business.

But had he been the one to corrupt her sister's file? Did he have any IT knowledge? Or did he have friends who were still within the Bureau who'd done that? And if so, why? Why on earth had such a thing been necessary at all? What were they trying to hide?

Cami decided that before arriving on his doorstep, she needed to delve deeper into Treverton's IT credentials and get an idea of whether or not he could have done it.

But before she could do that, her phone rang. The sudden buzzing caused her to jump because she'd been concentrating so hard.

It was Special Agent Connor on the line, from the FBI, and Cami felt a flash of guilt as she automatically connected her illicit activities with this call.

Did he know what she'd been doing? Was he calling to say he'd found her out? The timing was worrying to her. Of course, the other alternative was that he was letting her know about a new case. Those were the only two choices. There was no other reason why Connor would be calling her at all, let alone at five-thirty a.m.

It was time to find out.

Hoping it was the second of the two possibilities, she picked up the call. "Cami speaking."

"Cami, it's Connor here."

He didn't say he hoped that he hadn't woken her. Wasn't that what a normal person would say when calling at this hour? Unless, of course, he already knew that she was awake because he knew what she'd been doing.

"Morning, Connor," she said nervously.

"I need you in the office. Now. Can you get here in twenty minutes?" he asked.

Her heart accelerated even more. This was trouble, she sensed it.

"Twenty minutes? Sure, I can be there." She hesitated. "Is this . . . is this in connection with a new case?"

She had to know. She needed to be put out of her misery. But the line was dead. Connor had already cut the call.

Feeling the worry now flare inside her, Cami hustled for her wardrobe. She grabbed the FBI jacket and baseball cap that she'd been given on her first assignment and told to keep for the future, then called a cab.

The FBI office was a ten-minute ride away, which meant she had less than ten minutes to get ready within his timeframe, so she needed to hustle. She didn't want to be late for Connor. He'd sounded serious. Either she was in big trouble, or else this was a new case that she'd now be launched straight into. Neither was what she felt prepared for after a sleepless night.

Whichever it was, she told herself with a dark humor, at least it wouldn't be too much longer before she knew her fate.

CHAPTER THREE

Eighteen minutes later, Cami rushed up to the main entrance of the Boston FBI offices. She felt anxiety surging inside her. Most probably, she acknowledged, her sleep-deprived state wasn't helping.

She didn't know if she was about to be arrested or be given a challenging new case that would require brain power that her exhausted mind didn't have at that moment. Either way, things were far from ideal.

She rushed through security. Was it good or bad that Connor wasn't downstairs waiting? She didn't know. Early as it was, the offices were busy. Security was on duty, and a few agents were hurrying along the polished floors. There was an air of intensity, seriousness, and focus in the building.

Someone's laugh rang out from around the corner, reminding Cami that the FBI was not an establishment populated by machines or robots, but by actual humans. That made her feel a little better, although she then found dark thoughts of Agent Treverton looming in her mind again.

She hustled over to the elevator and headed upstairs, rushing along the corridor to Connor's office, checking the time as she reached the door.

Nineteen minutes since his call. She'd made it within his deadline.

The door was ajar, so Cami tapped on it just as a formality before stepping inside. Now, it was time. Now, she'd know.

And then, her eyes widened. Connor wasn't in the office. But turning around, with a surprised expression on his clean-cut face, was Ethan Myers.

He looked as pleased to see her as she did to see him. A grin spread across his features, his white teeth flashed, his brown eyes warmed.

"Hey, Cami!"

"Ethan!"

She liked Ethan, she really did. She felt there was a spark between them. In fact, Cami had to admit that as she'd gotten to know Ethan a little better, he'd done more than anyone else to change her opinion of the FBI. He was so sharp and driven, and he'd chosen to make a career move and become an agent. Cami had previously perceived the FBI as a bumbling, faceless, bureaucratic organization filled with incompetent and unmotivated people—thanks to her experience after Jenna had vanished.

But now, she understood Ethan's passion for his work and that he was highly motivated, as a bright, young guy bursting with talent, to fight crime and to be part of an organization that he thought restored order to society.

"I didn't know you were going to be here," she said.

"Me either, until half an hour ago. Connor called and asked me to come in. I guess it's a new case. But I don't know the details."

"Do you think it's a murder?" Seeing Ethan was sitting at the small, round table in the corner of the office, Cami headed over and took a seat opposite.

"I assume it is. Connor's in a meeting with Fraser."

Fraser was Connor's boss. So, it definitely sounded like a serious case had landed. For now, Cami felt as if she'd dodged a bullet.

"It's great to see you," Ethan said. "I've missed you on the team. You know, I have to say, I was kind of hoping an IT-related case would come up, seeing as you're on call for them."

"For a year," Cami said thoughtfully, remembering the terms of her agreement with the FBI, which had been contractually signed and sealed. But that didn't mean that they couldn't change it. She'd seen that they were capricious when it involved people being at their beck and call whose expertise they needed.

But with Ethan on the team, Cami had to admit that a year didn't seem like so long. In fact, it seemed doable. Reasonable.

"If Fraser's already here I guess it must be serious."

"Yes. I agree, but there's nothing we can do now but wait," Ethan said with a wry smile.

Cami scooted closer, leaning her elbows on the table. "You know what I was thinking?" she said, feeling nervous that she was going out on a limb here with this line of conversation. She hoped that it wasn't inappropriate, but since they had some time together, why not?

"No, I don't know. What were you thinking?" Ethan replied.

"I was wondering if you like metal music."

"Metal? Sure."

"There's one of my favorite bands in town—Hardcore Hearts. They're doing gigs. They don't do big concerts. They do smaller venues. Pubs, clubs, and the like. They've got a few venues lined up next week, and I wanted to go. Would you come with me?"

"I'd love to!" Cami felt excited that Ethan sounded totally genuine. He really sounded as if this concert would be the best idea in the world. "I love that kind of music and that kind of gig. It's a date."

Cami felt her heart quicken. It had taken a lot of courage to ask Ethan out, after their drinks date last week that he'd asked her on. She thought this relationship was getting somewhere, but it was still surprisingly scary for her to get close to anyone. She didn't trust easily. But she'd done it now. Going to see Hardcore Hearts was a date, and she was excited about it.

At that moment, footsteps approached, and they both scooted their chairs further away from each other, turning toward the door.

Special Agent Connor strode inside. His strong face looked serious. His dark, graying hair was neatly cut. He looked focused and determined, despite the early hour. He gave a nod of approval to see Cami and Ethan waiting.

"Morning," he said. "Thanks for getting here so fast."

"Morning," they chorused. Cami looked at him expectantly as he sat down and set a folder on the desk.

Connor didn't ask them how they were or indulge in any social pleasantries. That wasn't his style. He was all about facts, plans, and results. But he wasn't a cold man. Cami had realized that deep inside his seemingly rigid and uncaring persona, there was a streak of kindness.

Well-hidden sometimes, but there, nonetheless.

"We've got a new case," he said, and Cami felt a knot of tension inside her loosen just a little because his words had confirmed this wasn't trouble for her. But it didn't loosen too much. A new case meant she'd need to bring all her skills to the situation. She was under no illusions that this would be hard, challenging, and potentially dangerous.

"There have been two women killed in two days, both with the same MO, which is why the FBI has been called in," Connor said.

Cami glanced at Ethan, then looked at Connor again, waiting for more information. She hadn't heard of anything locally, although apart from last night's antics in the archives, she'd been buried in her studies, with final exams just around the corner. Although perhaps the crimes had been hushed up.

"Both of the victims were hit over the head and knocked unconscious before being drowned. One was drowned in Lake Michigan, the other in the dolphin pool at the Milwaukee aquarium."

Milwaukee. That explained it. It was in another state, not in Massachusetts at all, which is why it hadn't gotten onto her radar, Cami thought. The location reminded her that the FBI was not limited by state borders. Any crime, any emergency, demanded that the best agents for the job were deployed.

Ethan frowned. "In the dolphin pool? How's that possible? Was nobody else around, or what?"

"It seems that she got there after closing time and found her way in."

"Oh, okay." He nodded.

"Any link between the victims?" Cami asked, knowing from experience that this would be important.

"Nothing obvious in common. They lived in different areas and have no mutual colleagues or friends. However, both women were active online, and in fact, the first victim was an online celebrity, a content creator. The second was a make-up artist. So, there may be a link there, which is why you've been called in."

"Do we know it's a serial? Were there signatures left at the scenes?" Cami asked.

"Good question," Connor said. "And yes. There were signatures left at the scenes. At both scenes, a blue wristband was left. You know, those silicone wristbands you wear for charity, fundraisers, events, and so on?"

"Yes," Ethan said, nodding.

"One was left at each scene, with an earring pierced through it, the kind used in an ear piercing. Both of them had the same red bead. The FBI agent who looked at the scene wondered if it was somehow depicting a location pin, and again, this points to online expertise being needed."

"I guess it does," Cami said.

"One wristband was found near the body in the lake, and one was found in the dolphin pool. It seems that the killer might have thrown the bands down after killing the victims."

"But not on the bodies? They weren't wearing the bands?"

"No."

"A wristband with a pin? Something to do with a location, but the wristband itself? Why that? Why blue? Could there be more to it?" Cami wondered.

Connor stood up. "We're about to find out if there is more to it. We're going to the airport now, leaving for Milwaukee, to view the murder scenes and start investigating."

"We are? Now?" Startled, Cami jumped to her feet.

"Yes. We're being brought in to assist the local field office, and they want us to start immediately."

Cami swallowed. She'd better come up with something valuable if she was now flying to Milwaukee.

"Ethan, you hold down the fort here," Connor directed him. "I know you're heading out with Fraser's other team later on the trafficking case, but in the meantime, I want you to start looking into the victims' backgrounds and see if you can pick up any common factors the police might have missed, since the second murder was yesterday evening, so it's still very recent. As for us, we need to get going. It's a two-hour flight, and the sooner we get there, the sooner we can start to figure out what's going on."

He strode out with Cami rushing behind, barely having time to turn and wave at Ethan, who waved back before hustling to his office.

Location pins, blue armbands, water. There were only vague connections so far.

But Cami was already thinking ahead, wondering how this killer had known the victims were going to be where they were.

After closing time in a dolphin pool? That wasn't exactly an obvious place to find a murder victim. She thought she knew where that was pointing and felt eager to see if her theory was correct.

CHAPTER FOUR

Cami's eyes flew open as the plane touched down in Milwaukee. She'd been out like a light for the entire flight, so exhausted from her online activities last night that she couldn't even remember takeoff. She cast a guilty glance at Connor, wondering if he'd noticed. Hopefully he thought she was just a good sleeper on flights.

But he cast a knowing glance at her. "Busy time last night?"

She looked down.

"You'd better not be in the habit of burning the midnight oil too often," he warned. "You can't predict when cases will come along, and there won't always be a flight to catch up with sleep. We have a lot to do today. This case is urgent. When we fly into a different state, there's always more expected from us, and faster."

I should have known he'd have seen how exhausted I was, Cami thought wryly. It seemed nothing got past her part-time boss and investigation partner. Though not the sharpest when it came to IT, he didn't miss a trick when it came to human behavior and nuances.

They'd occupied seats in the front row, and as soon as the door was opened, Connor hustled out, with Cami following close behind. He got on his phone as he strode toward the exit, and cutting the call, made straight for a police officer waiting beyond. This man was in his thirties, Cami guessed. He had closely cropped brown hair and a worried expression.

"I'm Detective Welsh. Morning, Agent Connor."

“Morning, Detective,” Connor greeted him politely. “This is the IT expert, Cami Lark,” he introduced her.

“If it's okay with you, Agent Connor, we can go straight to the aquarium," he said.

"Sure, let's do that."

“It’s good to have you on board. This case looks like it’s going to blow up in our faces. Politically, I mean. With one body discovered at a city aquarium and the other belonging to one of our major social media influencers, this killer is causing panic already.”

“When was the second body discovered?” Connor asked.

"It was discovered very early this morning when the cleaners opened up to clean the pool. The aquarium is now shut down, and people are very unhappy about it," Welsh told them.

Connor shook his head. “It’s a worrying situation,” he agreed.

They walked out of the airport to a police car that was parked in the pick-up zone. Welsh got in and opened it for them. Cami headed straight for the back seat, and Connor got in the front. He passed her the files.

"You'd better have a look at these en route," he said. "Familiarize yourself with the case."

He'd obviously done that earlier, on the plane, while she'd been snoozing. Feeling thoroughly guilty about her overnight activities, Cami took the folders and read up on her newest case, wanting to take in all the details now. Connor was speaking to Welsh, who was updating him about general crime in the area as they drove. Tuning that conversation out, Cami did as she'd been tasked and focused on the pages in front of her.

Victim number one, Leanne Hind, had been found on the shores of Lake Michigan on a hiking trail a few miles out of suburban Milwaukee. Reading further, Cami saw that Leanne was tall, blonde, and pretty. She was twenty-five years old and was a social media influencer who had seemed to lead a high profile and well-sponsored life. She represented a few major companies and brands, and also did work for the Milwaukee tourism board, promoting sites and highlights within her home city.

Patti Browne, the second victim, was older. Blonde, round-faced, and assertive looking, she was in her late thirties, Cami saw. She was a make-up artist who did special effects and movie work, and she had a very big online following. She'd been found dead at the aquarium early this morning, but her car had been in the outside parking lot overnight, according to the parking attendant.

"Both of these victims lived their lives very much online," Cami said aloud.

Connor's head turned instantly, and he glanced back at her. "Is that so?"

"Yes. Leanne was an influencer, so her activities were all shared online. And Patti shared wherever possible. I guess that's how she boosted her clientele. She was very clever about marketing herself and her make-up effects."

Cami paged further, scrolling through the online world where both these victims had been so active. Were there any other clues to be found?

"It looks as if Leanne used to pin her location regularly," Cami said. "Like, every time she went anywhere."

"So, if people had been following her online, they'd know where she was?" Connor's voice was sharp. It was clear that he was making the connection, just as she'd done.

"Correct," Cami agreed. "I think she did it for her fans and for her clients."

"So, now we know there's a potential link between the killer and the victim. If the killer followed her online, he would have known she's going to be in that area, and he could have waited for her there."

"It would seem so," Cami said.

"I'm saying 'he' until we know more. We can't rule out a strong female killer."

"Absolutely," Welsh agreed.

She'd been so absorbed in the files that she'd barely noticed the drive from the airport to the aquarium's entrance. Already, they were driving in. It was nearly nine in the morning, and she saw that this crime had created a minor commotion in the area.

Crime scene tape barricaded the entrance, seemingly drawing crowds of onlookers who were standing outside, looking shocked and curious.

Connor parked as close as he could, and they got out. Detective Welsh led the way. He passed the throng of people quickly, turning when he heard a shouted question.

"Any leads so far? The Milwaukee News wants to know!"

"We're following up on all leads. The FBI is here on site. We'll be holding a conference for the media as soon as there's any updates," Welsh replied calmly, but Cami could see the stress in his face as he turned and headed on.

"Morning. FBI has arrived," he greeted the police officer who was guarding the entrance.

"Go through, please. Everyone is still by the dolphin pool. Including the aquarium manager and the mayor," the police officer said, sounding less than enthusiastic about the political interference that was already descending.

The aquarium entrance looked bright and cheery, with vivid signage and paintings of fish and dolphins on the outer walls. It didn't seem the location for a crime scene, Cami thought, sensing how out of place this murder felt. *Why here?* she wondered. She could understand why a killer might have lain in wait on a hiking trail, but at an aquarium after hours?

Shoulder to shoulder with Officer Welsh, Connor strode through. Cami followed behind, along a paved path lined with plants, passing more walls with fishy murals. She hadn't expected a large crowd at the aquarium poolside, but as they entered the pool area, she saw that there was a lot of people at the scene.

There were first responders and a pathologist on site, she saw, guessing that retrieving the body from the deep pool must have been a difficult and specialized process. In fact, the body was still there. A stretcher, with water dripping below it, was near the edge of the pool. A pathologist was bending over it, clearly conducting an initial on-site examination.

A few men in business suits were arguing with a police officer. As they approached, the argument paused.

Everyone turned to look at Connor. Nobody looked thrilled to see him. Welsh hastily made the introductions.

"Morning. This is Special Agent Connor and IT expert Cami Lark from the FBI." Turning to the other group, he said, "This is Mayor Maree and his advisers. And this is Bill Sands, the aquarium manager, and his team who runs the aquarium for the city."

"We need to open up," Sands insisted, frowning at Connor. "This has already been a disaster for us. We've plowed a fortune into refurbishing it. I know how tragic this is, but you guys need to see things our way. We have a lot to do. We have to clean out the pool, change the water, recirculate it, and get things ready. And we can't do any of that if you keep putting a hold on our activities here."

"We've been doing our best, sir," Welsh said defensively. "This is part of a major, serial crime. We have a complete lack of witnesses on the scene." He sounded annoyed as if the aquarium should have been better staffed or better secured.

"We're not equipped to deal with surprise visitors after hours," the manager retorted defensively. "People can read notice boards, can't they?"

"Law enforcement is supposed to work for the city," Mayor Maree frowned. "Not to intentionally try to delay us."

"We'll get you open up again as soon as we're able to," Connor said briskly. "Now, let's take a look at what we have here."

He glanced up at the balcony overhanging the pool, and Cami guessed he was wondering if the victim might have been attacked there. Maybe she'd fled up there when the killer had approached her and fallen into the pool. In that case, how had he found her?

Quickly, she scrolled through Patti's social media to see if she'd mentioned where she was going to be.

And she had, Cami saw. She'd written, *"En route to the aquarium next! Going to get some photo ops with the dolphins, ready for my Sea Theme make-up effects launches! Wait till you see them. Or 'Sea' them!"*

So, she'd advertised her arrival here. If someone had been following her online, they would have known she'd be coming.

Had they waited here for her? Or had they followed her from elsewhere? Since she'd only posted this update late in the afternoon, this couldn't have been planned that far ahead, unless she'd mentioned it earlier on in the week. But what if someone had been tracking her more recently, and had used this opportunity to move in for the kill?

In that case, Cami thought, *it would be important to know where she was beforehand. Was there anything to be found?*

She checked back in Patti's social media. And then, she walked quickly over to Connor, interrupting what looked like the beginning of a less-than-civil argument between law enforcement and aquarium and city management.

"I've seen that Patti had a meeting before she came here. It was about twenty miles away. She mentioned the aquarium visit online just before she attended the meeting. Do you think that someone from that meeting could have followed her here?" she asked.

CHAPTER FIVE

"Could someone from the earlier meeting have followed Patti to the aquarium? That's a definite possibility," Connor said, and Cami heard the approval in his voice. "Let's take a look at this meeting. Who was it with? What can we find out about it?"

Moving away from the argument with the officials, he walked over to stand in the shade with Cami and looked down at what she'd found.

"Okay, it seems that it was a presentation with a group of people from a local arts club," Connor said, thoughtfully reading through the available information. There was no shortage of that, Cami saw. Patti had lived her life very much in the public eye. She was used to advertising her presence and her destination everywhere she went.

"It's great for promotion, sure. But advertising your whereabouts constantly is risky at the same time," Connor muttered. "Now, at this recent meeting, she met with eight people who all look to be strangers to her. Did one of them decide to follow her, or else get ahead of her and wait?"

Cami wondered if Patti had been unlucky enough to attract the attention of a killer in this meeting.

"We need to take a closer look at those eight, with the potential to commit both the murders in mind. We're looking for anyone who might have gone on to the aquarium after the meeting. And also, we're looking for anyone who would have been able to go out on the hiking trails yesterday and murder Leanne. Either of those connection points will mean a reason to look more closely."

"I can work on that," Cami said. She was pleased that Connor was so determined to follow up on the possibility she'd suggested.

"Go ahead and start on the social media activities and see what you can find," Connor suggested. "Look for anything that might give us a lead. Meanwhile, I'll go talk with the police and try to get a timeframe in place for the reopening of this aquarium." Sounding resigned, he strode back to the fray, leaving Cami to research the meeting.

It had been with members of the Milwaukee Art and Drama Society, she saw. Eight people from the society had attended the make-up presentation Patti had given. She had scheduled additional short meetings with two of the eight, after the main meeting. So, the society had kept her busy all afternoon.

Now, who were these eight, and was there any way to track their whereabouts?

She was able to find a group photo online, taken with Patti at the meeting, that gave her all the names and identities. Patiently, working as fast as she could, Cami matched up each one with their own social media profile.

She guessed that a killer would not have publicly checked into a murder site, so she wasn't even going to waste time looking there. Rather, she needed to look for other ways. Sneaky ways.

Absorbed in her task, she tuned out the debate a few yards away, only vaguely aware that it seemed to be getting resolved and that they were finally reaching agreement. At any rate, the voices were less loud.

Even though she knew the police had already done some initial work here and found no links, Cami did a quick check to see if there was any connection at all between these victims from a social media perspective. But she could find none, beyond the fact that they had many thousands of friends, connections, and followers on different platforms, and that some of these were going to overlap. But no close friends or direct work connections were shared.

The two women were different in age. They had different jobs. The only common factor was that both of them were high profile on social media and had big public followings, with probably a few thousand in common.

From the initial eight people that Patti had met with, she'd ruled out five as having been obviously busy at the times the murders occurred. These five had all gone straight on to a play rehearsal after the meeting with Patti—as a subsequent photo caption stated.

Three remained: the society's vice president and two of the members. Coincidentally, these three were the only men in the group. The five women were cleared.

As she looked more closely, Cami's attention focused more sharply on one of the men.

He was the society's vice president: Nick Simmel. Nick attracted her attention because he lived very close to the area where Leanne had died. His address was just a couple of miles from the point where she'd been found drowned.

Nick was thirty-eight years old and single. He lived alone. But what intrigued her was that he was one of those who followed both Leanne and Patti on various platforms. In fact, he'd connected with both quite recently. That, for her, was a red flag.

Had he targeted them with the intention of going on a killing spree? Being a single man, a loner, did that make it more likely? She wasn't sure, but she decided to check out his whereabouts after the meeting yesterday.

Cami opened his social media profile and started looking around. She could see that this wasn't going to be easy. Anyone who had killed these two women was not going to be advertising their guilt on social media. They'd be hiding their tracks as best they could.

But she had to try.

She couldn't find anything on social media linking him to the aquarium, but a little more research showed her his car's make and color. It was a silver Ford SUV and digging deeper, Cami found the number plate.

She wasn't sure if this research would get her anywhere, but she did remember that there had been a camera at the entrance to the main parking lot that was used by the aquarium, the dolphin pool, the gift shop, and a small coffee shop.

Was there a possibility that his car could have been captured on that camera?

"Connor, I might have something here," she said, seeing that he'd finally finished the discussion and was striding back toward her.

"You do? What have you found?"

"Nick Simmel was one of the people at the meeting. He connected with both the victims recently. He lives close to where Leanne was killed. And I wonder if he might have followed Patti here. I have his car's number plate. If he used the main parking lot, then there might be camera records."

"Let's ask the aquarium manager. Given that they are so keen to open again, I'm sure they'll be willing to show us that footage immediately," Connor agreed.

He called out to the two men, who were busy walking toward the office.

"We need to see the parking camera footage from yesterday afternoon. Can you take us in and show us?"

As Connor had predicted, the aquarium manager was now all eagerness.

"Sure. Of course I can. The sooner we can get everything wrapped up and reopened, the better. Come this way."

“I’d actually like you to send us all that footage,” Connor said, clearly thinking ahead. Cami thought this was a good idea. Although hundreds of cars would have headed in and out of that large, busy parking lot, it would provide them with a way to check if the killer had been there—assuming Nick wasn’t the killer. But if they were lucky, he was.

As they headed into the aquarium buildings, Connor was already on the phone to Ethan.

"Do me a favor," he asked. "Background check. Guy called Nick Simmel. I'll send you through his details. See if there's anything on him, will you?"

Then, following the manager, he strode through the blue-painted doorway, down a short passage, and into another office with walls decorated with fishy friezes. Cami followed close behind.

"The camera feed is on a computer that's through here," the manager said, pacing to the far end.

The old-looking monitor was placed on a desk in the corner, next to a few spare cables and an empty fish tank. Cami immediately thought it was just as well that the aquarium manager had been agreeable, because this was old technology—basic, simple, and ironically, difficult to hack.

But the manager bent over the machine and within a minute, the footage was playing.

Cami took another look at the number plate and then, with the digits firmly in her mind, turned back to the screen. She felt her pulse quicken. This might get them the lead they needed. There had to be a reason why Nick Simmel had linked up with both the victims so recently.

"There's Patti's number plate," Connor said thoughtfully. "This is playing in reverse. So, he didn't follow her here. He didn't come afterward. But did he get here earlier?"

Now, they were all leaning forward, intent on solving this puzzle. Car after car turned silently in and out of the lot, in the footage, which was black and white with the occasional wavy line.

And then, she saw it. She and Connor drew in a sharp breath at exactly the same time. It was the car they wanted. The silver Ford. Turning into the aquarium just half an hour before Patti had arrived.

"It's a clear link," Connor said decisively. "He was there, on site. He has had contact with both victims. We need to find Nick Simmel, now."

CHAPTER SIX

The stars were bright above him as he looked up to the darkened ceiling. Outside, it was a sunny morning. But inside the planetarium, it was night. Deepest, darkest night.

The lost man had come here hoping for guidance. Hoping that he might be able to use the stars to find them, these people he had lost. Surely, it was possible? With the alignment of the stars, he might be able to map his route.

"I feel so lonely. So lost," he murmured, but softly. He didn't want to interrupt the voice of the announcer as he calmly explained the planetary movements and highlighted the constellations in the twinkling lights above.

He tried his best to fix their positions in his mind, feeling panic rise, because they were so complex, so difficult to remember. But they must be able to help him somehow, to find his way back.

Then he gasped as all the twinkling lights went off, leaving the blackness above him blank and absolute.

"On its own, the human eye finds it difficult to fix in one place. Especially without visual references to help. And here is proof of this."

In the black ceiling, one pinprick light appeared.

"Watch this star."

The light shone a few moments and then it went out. After another few moments of blackness, the star reappeared, but it was now a good distance to the right, the lost man saw.

"This is in the same position as last time," the announcer continued implacably. "But to the human eye, it will appear to have moved, because without any light to focus on, our vision constantly moves and adjusts, and our eyes don't remain looking at the same place we saw."

The light winked out again. Then it reappeared, but higher up in the ceiling. Except it wasn't higher, the lost man realized, panic now blooming inside him. It was in the same place it had been, but he wasn't seeing it so. He was incapable of seeing it that way because he was lost, he was disoriented, his vision was faulty, and it was going to prevent him from ever finding his way back again, with or without stars to help him. Nothing could help him. What chance did he have?

Taking a deep, panicked breath, he scrambled up from his seat, stumbling in the dark, pushing past the other people. He tripped over their legs, hearing their annoyed murmurs but not caring. He was blind in the absolute blackness, but knew that he needed to get out, that he couldn't stay in this prison anymore, that this lesson on the heavens was not going to help him.

"Excuse me, please. Excuse me."

He pushed past them all, the panic rising, because he couldn't see. He couldn't see this way. He couldn't see at all.

Pushing open the heavy exit door, he stumbled out into the carpeted lobby of the planetarium. There was light now, from overhead and from outside, searing his eyes, impossibly bright after the cool darkness within. He was breathing hard. Memories were looming in his mind, unwanted and terrible. How would he ever find them? He'd gone in there hoping for direction, but he'd come out with a harsh lesson that emphasized how frail and weak he was, how weak they all were.

He checked his phone. Normality seeped back. He had an appointment later this afternoon. He had ordinary things to do in his ordinary life. And yet, the loneliness, the panic, and the sense of terrible disorientation and loss still flared.

"Did you enjoy it?" a motherly-looking woman with curly, red hair asked, bustling out. It seemed that the show was over. He'd only skipped the last couple of minutes after his hasty escape.

"Yes," he lied, with a tight smile. "Yes, I did. It was . . . informative."

"It's interesting, isn't it?" she persisted, clearly wanting to chat. "The way our eyes play tricks on us. We see what we expect to see."

"Yes."

"And how we're different from other creatures who can see things in the dark. So, perhaps we need to change our expectations."

"Yes." He nodded, wondering how much longer she was going to keep speaking to him, because he couldn't handle a conversation right now. He felt as if he was about to crack wide open inside.

Thankfully, with a cheerful smile, she finally turned away. He was left with his own thoughts, his own terror, because he was no longer seeing the stars, but instead, he was remembering the colossal black emptiness of space, the emptiness that surrounded this miniscule planet, and he felt his breath catch in his throat at the thought of it.

He took his phone out. It had been turned off for the show, but now he turned it on. He checked all his updates, making sure he hadn't missed anything.

He caught his breath. There was a possibility here. There was! This might be more than a coincidence.

He stared down at his screen. She was here. Definitely here. One of the ones he was seeking. She must have arrived late. He'd thought she wouldn't be here at all. But now, she was.

And then, looking up, he saw her out of the corner of his eye.

It was the merest flash, but it was enough for familiarity. For hope. This could mean he was able to find just one of those he sought.

She was tall and curvaceous, with a thick head of blonde hair tied back in a ponytail. She was wearing a pink top and carrying a brown leather purse over her shoulder. He couldn't remember the top, but that must be his own mind playing tricks on him. He was sure he remembered the purse.

With hope flaring inside him now, he turned in her direction.

"Mother?" he whispered, not daring to say the word aloud.

Was it her? Now, he couldn't tell, because the woman had turned and was heading swiftly out of the planetarium.

He caught a glimpse of her face as she turned, a flash of her profile, but it was too far away to see properly.

And then, she was gone.

She was going to leave him behind. She didn't want him to speak to her. He was going to lose her all over again, and the pain was suddenly too intense to bear. He moved to follow her, but the people around him were getting in the way, and it was a struggle to move forward among the crowds.

"Excuse me." He moved to the side to get around the couple blocking his way. "Excuse me. Please."

He had to follow her. He had to find out if it was her. Or if it was only a trick of his eyes. He could have been wrong, but he didn't think he was.

Finally, he managed to get past them, heading now for the exit.

"Mother?" he called again, hurrying after her. But she was already out into the daylight that seemed too bright after the darkness. But he knew where she was going. He already knew. There was no need to panic, he told himself. He could find her. She was following her plotted course, just like the stars themselves.

However, there was a need to follow. He wanted to see her some more, that was why.

There she was, hurrying away, weaving through the people on the sidewalk, her ponytail bouncing. His heart was pounding. He was even surer now that it was her, and he felt desperate to find her and be with her, to reconnect with a part of the life he'd lost.

He raced along, dodging people, muttering an apology as he bumped into a woman with a small child. He raced along, the hope growing inside him, because he knew that he remembered her purse. It was familiar. He was sure of it.

He knew that there wasn't much time. He had places to be this afternoon. But there should be enough time.

The woman turned down a side street. He veered after her, trying to contain the confusion in his mind, trying his best to keep sight of this very special person who might just be one of those he thought he would never see again.

She climbed into her car, and he glanced down at his phone again, feeling a weird sense of confidence that overrode his earlier anxiety.

Even if he lost her now, he knew he could find her again, because he had done his homework. He reached into his pocket, feeling the blue wristband he had there, ready for the moment ahead.

He smiled, feeling suddenly less nervous and a cold sureness inside.

Their stars were going to align.

CHAPTER SEVEN

Nick Simmel lived in a small apartment block in a residential suburb of Milwaukee, a mile to the south of where Leanne's body had been found. Sitting in the front seat of the police car that she and Connor had been loaned, Cami looked eagerly ahead as the road they wanted came into view.

There was the apartment block. Park Villas. Nick Simmel lived at number six.

The villas were located in a garden setting, spaced out around grounds that included a basketball court and a swimming pool.

"I don't have a recorded workplace for him," Connor said, getting out of the car. "I see something's just come through from Ethan."

His eyebrows raised as he read it. "It's not a workplace. It's a record. I see that Nick Simmel has had a restraining order filed against him in the past by a previous girlfriend. That could be significant."

Cami's eyes narrowed. The man was a stalker, for sure. Now, they needed to find out how far he'd taken things.

Connor strode up the garden path to villa number six and rapped hard on the door. Cami waited, feeling anxious now that they were about to come face to face with a suspected killer. She had to stop herself from shifting nervously from foot to foot.

It didn't seem like Nick Simmel was here. Perhaps there was a place of work where he'd gone, and it wasn't yet on the police database. Or perhaps he was hiding inside.

Was there anything she could use to help out that way? Cami looked around, her eyes scouring the area for any smart devices, any cameras, any sign of anything that she might be able to commandeer to take a peek inside, or else to flush Nick out.

She didn't see anything. But as she looked at the pool in the apartment block's grounds, Cami noticed there was a man inside it, swimming laps with a fit, rhythmic stroke.

He had dark hair. That, she could see, slick and wet as it was. The man they were looking for had dark hair.

"Connor," she muttered. "Do you think he might be over there?"

Water had been an integral part of both these crimes, and now the man she thought was Nick Simmel was swimming in the pool. *Was this possibly indicative of an obsession?* Cami wondered.

Connor swung around and took a closer look at the pool. "Let's go and see," he said.

He strode away from the door, through the grounds, and eased open the gate in the swimming pool fence.

The man was at the far end of the pool, just busy completing a lap. He paused mid-stroke when he saw them and grasped the side of the pool.

"Nick Simmel?" Connor called out.

Now that they were closer, Cami was sure it was their man. She recognized the slightly hooded eyes and the shape of his chin that she'd seen in the group photo. Now, he'd paused his swim. He was watching them, and he looked tense and wary.

"Nick Simmel, FBI here. We need to ask you some questions," Connor insisted. He paced over to the edge of the pool and began moving around to where Nick was now frozen in place, gripping the side.

But as Connor walked, Cami saw, to her surprise, that Nick was moving too. He kicked off from the edge of the pool and swam into the center. There, he stood, shoulder deep in the water, glancing nervously at Connor.

"Nick, we need to ask you questions," Connor said.

Nick shook his head. "I'm not prepared to answer."

What? Cami's eyebrows rose in disbelief. This man was hiding out in plain sight in the middle of a pool, refusing to answer questions. And out of reach of the police.

She'd never heard of such a thing. Was this really how people behaved when they were faced with the FBI and clearly had something to hide?

Connor's resigned expression told Cami that this was all too normal in what she guessed was never a typical day's work.

"You can't hide in the middle of a public pool," he said. "You need to give us answers."

"I'm not prepared to answer any questions," Nick repeated. "I'm not willing to speak to you."

Connor shook his head. "That's not how this works," he said. "This is a murder investigation. If you refuse to cooperate, you'll be committing offenses already."

"I'm not hiding anything," Nick said, now sounding scared, taking another step back.

"Maybe you don't want to answer the questions," Connor said. "Maybe you think you can avoid the questions. But you are obviously worried about the questioning. That's clear to us. So now, we have even more reason to need answers."

"I'm not coming out," he said.

Cami stared at him, wondering exactly what the FBI protocol was in this situation. They weren't going to walk away. That was clear in every determined line of Connor's face. But at the same time, their suspect was refusing to talk.

"Every day on the job, you see something that further reinforces your opinion of the general public's capability for idiocy," Connor muttered.

Then, to Cami's surprise and amusement, Connor stripped off his jacket and removed his belt with the gun on it. He took his boots off and unclipped the handcuffs off his gun belt.

"Don't touch the gun, or let anyone touch it, until I'm out of here," he said, handing Cami the belt.

Then, with a resigned sigh, Connor strode to the water's edge, grasping his handcuffs.

He took a deep breath and then, with more athleticism than Cami had expected, he dove in. With a mighty splash, Connor cut the water's surface, swimming determinedly in Nick's direction.

With a startled cry, Nick began half swimming, half wading away. But Connor was gaining, doing a messy but speedy crawl stroke.

Cami ran around the edge of the pool in the direction Nick was heading, intending to cut him off if it was needed. But it wasn't needed. Connor grasped Nick's arm and then, as Nick began chopping and kicking out at him, a splashy fight ensued.

"You're not getting away, and we're not spending any more time in this damned swimming pool," Connor threatened through gritted teeth. If he hadn't already been thoroughly wet from the dive, he would have been by the time he'd finished wrestling with the struggling suspect. Nick was writhing and twisting, trying his damnedest to get away, but Cami saw with a skip of her heart that one of the handcuffs was already in place. Nick was captured, and now, Connor was dragging him the rest of the way to the side.

"You can't do this! You're infringing my rights."

"Have you heard of failure to obey? It's an offense."

"I've—Ow!" Nick protested, with a cry, as Connor dragged him up the pool's steps.

Connor's face was set. "We can do this the easy way or the hard way," he said. "But we are leaving this pool. I'm not questioning you waist-deep in water."

Cami was waiting, setting the gun belt down carefully out of reach before rushing forward to grasp one of Nick's cool, dripping arms. Nick was gasping for breath, and his eyes were wide with shock, but Cami and Connor's combined efforts had him onto the pavement before he had time to realize what was happening.

Connor got the other cuff behind him and clamped it shut. Then he pushed Nick's shoulders down until he reluctantly folded into a sitting position on the pavement by the side of the pool.

"There have been two murders in the past two days. You connected with both the victims on social media, and you arrived at the aquarium, where one victim was subsequently killed, soon after meeting with her. So now, I have questions. And it's time for answers," Connor threatened, in tones that told Cami no further resistance would be allowed.

CHAPTER EIGHT

The stars were sending him along the right route at last. The lost man felt sure of it. This was the direction he needed. The path he should follow. He saw where she was going, this woman who he thought was his mother. And now, all he needed to do was to arrive.

"It's all going to work out," he whispered as he walked away from the planetarium, following the destination he knew was mapped out for him. This was what he needed. At last, it was all going to be okay.

"Things are working out for you?" a man asked as he headed to his car, walking fast and purposefully.

The lost man barely glanced at him. This man meant nothing in his life; he was a nobody. He had dark hair. He was in his forties. He noticed these facts almost in passing.

"Yes," he said. "Things are working out."

"I'm glad," the man said, and the lost man realized that he was speaking to him. He looked up and saw that the man, a stranger, had stopped walking. He was watching him and smiling.

"It's good to see someone who's talking positive," the man said. "Too many people seem to spend their whole lives looking at the bad side of things."

"I try not to do that," the lost man said.

"I myself had a loss recently," the other man explained.

"You did?" The lost man looked suspiciously at him. What was this about?

"I lost my wallet. Unfortunately. So, I was wondering if you have any cash on you? I need some, just to get home, that's all." He smiled hopefully at the lost man.

The lost man told himself that there wasn't anything wrong with this. He was only being asked for a small amount of money. He could spare a few dollar bills. There was nothing wrong with a small act of kindness. But at the same time, he knew that he could not afford to be noticed. What if this man prevented him from doing what he needed to do? It would be better to shut this conversation down, right now.

"I don't have any cash," the lost man said. It wasn't true, but he felt the need to emphasize.

"That's too bad," the man said sadly, still watching him.

"It's really not a lot," the man said, following after. "A twenty would do it. I'm really not asking for much."

"I don't have any cash at all," the lost man said.

"There, you see?" The man sounded angry now. "You're just like all the others, thinking only of yourself."

"So be it," the lost man snapped.

Needing to cut this conversation short, now panicking that he was running out of time, he jumped into his car. Starting it up, he hit the gas, causing the other man to jump out of the way as he sped in the direction of the main street.

His mother—he was sure that it was her—was calling to him, and he knew now exactly where she would be. He had no time to waste. He was not interested in helping strangers who were more like thieves. That man could have ruined his plans. For all he knew, he could even have been an undercover cop. Paranoia surged.

Trying to tamp it down, reassuring himself that things were still going to be okay, the lost man accelerated in the direction he knew he had to go. South. He felt as if the coordinates were pulling him that way.

"I can see you," he told the now-invisible stars. "I can feel you. I can reach out and touch you."

He would get to her this time. He was sure of it. He was on the right path, finally, heading towards the place where he knew she would be. The lost man felt short of breath and excited. He was on the way to finding her. He was convinced of it. He sped along the main road, slowing as he turned into a side road. It would be unwise to draw attention to himself. He had to be careful and remember not to do anything that might delay his all-important task. His mission. What he had to do to save himself.

"I'm getting near," he told the stars. "I can feel it."

He was so close now. He was almost there. Everything was going to work out this time. He could feel it.

He parked nearby, but not too near, because he knew that there was always the chance that he was wrong and that things would not go as planned. If he was arrested or locked away, he couldn't finish his mission.

He checked the street. It was quiet, with only a few houses nearby. If anyone saw him, they'd think he was a neighbor coming to visit someone.

Casually, he leaned back into the car and took the walking stick from the back seat. He didn't think he would need it because he was sure that, this time, he was right and that the person he was expecting was alive and waiting. There would be no need for the stick, which he washed so carefully in the water after those unfortunate times when he had to use it.

His breath was coming fast as he strolled along the sidewalk, heading for her house, her presence seeming to draw him there.

"Mother," he said under his breath.

He reached the house. This was where she was. Now, at last, he could see her clearly.

Keeping low, he crept out of sight of the street, rounding a wall into the back yard.

"I'm coming," he whispered, feeling a terrible eagerness erupt inside him. "I'm here. I'm in the right place. I've found you at last, and now I can save you."

He looked in through the window, his mouth dry. And there she was.

But it was not her! Disappointment thudded in his heart, together with a sense of doom. He'd been so sure, so very sure that it was her. And it wasn't. Now that he was seeing her more clearly, he realized his mistake. This woman's face was completely different. She was younger than his mother.

He'd made a stupid mistake. He wasn't in the right place. He'd arrived here by accident. He couldn't believe it. In fact, he had no idea what to do now that it felt as if his whole world had collapsed.

He felt dizzy with horror. The stick fell from his hand. He couldn't believe he'd made an error like this. He'd ruined everything. He'd been so sure. It was all in pieces now. What he had needed and longed for was beyond his grasp again.

"No," he muttered.

He tried to think the way he had to think. To make his brain work. What had he done wrong? Why had he got it wrong? How could such a mistake have happened?

Guilt pounded in his heart. He'd been so sure. He'd been so positive. And he'd made such a big mistake in not recognizing his own mother. He couldn't have been more wrong. He felt as if he should abandon all hope.

"No," he said again. "No, I can't believe it has to be this way. I can't believe this is how it's all going to end."

He was silent, looking around him at the quiet suburban scene. As he looked, the hidden part of him in the back of his mind was searching to make sure nobody had noticed him. The lost man felt that the hidden part was about to play an important role.

"I'm not beaten yet," he told himself. "I'm not beaten until I give up. And I'm not going to give up. Not yet."

He took a breath, trying to stay calm. He had to think. He'd got it wrong, but obviously, there was something that he had missed. Something that he had done wrong. There must be something he could do to reverse the situation. To fix it.

And then, once again, the light seemed to go on in his brain. Of course! He must do what he had done the last two times. The hidden part of his mind was sending messages that he understood now. Suddenly that weird, cold clarity was back in his mind, pushing him into action. This was nothing but an imposter, like the others had been. This entity, this stranger, was stealing his mother's place in the world. And just as he'd done the last time, he needed to cleanse the world of her. That way, his mother would have the chance to return. The steps of the ritual he would have to follow came back into his mind, clear and precise.

Of course. He'd been confused for a moment but now the way ahead was clear, and he knew exactly what he had to do.

Smiling, picking up the stick with a new resolve, he headed toward the home's back door.

CHAPTER NINE

Without a doubt, Nick Simmel was guilty, Cami sensed. The timing of his arrival at the aquarium was surely no coincidence. And he had a record of stalking and a previous restraining order against him.

He must be their killer. She felt certain of it.

But as she watched the dripping man, his face twitching and a towel roughly draped over his shoulders, Cami knew that suspicion alone was not enough and that Connor would now have to seek concrete proof from him.

Connor guided him, none too sympathetically, to one of the plastic deck chairs and sat him down on a cushion. Cami ran over to the cupboard near the pool, where she saw a few spare towels were folded, and brought back one for Connor. He was dripping, too, as he sat down on the deck chair opposite. But he barely seemed aware of it. All his focus was on the suspect.

"You were at the meeting with Patti Browne yesterday," he said. "She met with your arts and drama club."

Nick looked nervously at Connor. "Yes, we . . . we did meet with her," he stammered, looking cold now, as well as nervous.

"And then you came to the aquarium? Knowing she would be there?"

"I didn't come to meet her. I wasn't following her."

"You didn't? Then why are you here? What business did you have at the aquarium?"

Nick shook his head. "It was a coincidence," he said. "I was at the aquarium for an appointment. I didn't check who was there, and I had no idea Patti would be there."

"An appointment? With who?"

Nick was looking increasingly flustered. "I'm not a killer," he said. "I'm not trying to find victims. I'm trying to get my life back on track. Change direction. I had a meeting with my life coach nearby."

"At the aquarium?"

Nick looked down, shaking his head. "I was early for the meeting, so I stopped off there. Our meeting was at a coffee shop."

"You knew that Patti Browne would be here. You must have known."

Nick looked down. He had known, Cami was utterly sure.

Connor's voice was relentless. "Either you tell us the full truth now, or we are arresting you on suspicion of this murder."

"I—okay, I thought she was a very special woman. Attractive. I wanted to see her again. And yes, she did say she was going to be there for the dolphin feeding. I'm very shy. I don't have good social skills. I wanted to be near her. But I didn't want to intrude. I didn't want to risk her thinking I might be some kind of stalker." His voice was high and shaky.

A stalker was exactly what he was, Cami thought, confused by his denial.

"I thought maybe it would work if I arrived and coincidentally met up with her. But I left before she did because she had an extra meeting with a couple of others from the drama group, to discuss one of the upcoming performances. Then I heard that there was a big crash on the highway. I didn't see her and guessed she'd been delayed. So, it didn't work out. I left after the dolphin feeding and went on to meet my life coach. I knew I should just forget about her."

Cami looked over at Connor and saw that he was regarding Nick with narrowed eyes. He looked suspicious of Nick's story.

"Did you know Leanne Hind?"

"Is she the other woman who was killed? That happened near here, I think. We have fields and trails nearby, by the lake. It was there, wasn't it?"

"Did you know her?"

"No, but I knew of her. I thought she was very beautiful. I followed her on all her social media when she posted the other day about our area. She said she was going to be highlighting some of the walks and trails. I thought that was amazing."

"So, you say that's when you followed her? Were you aware of her movements? That she was coming out here to your area the day before yesterday?"

"No," Nick said, but Cami thought it might as well have been a yes.

"Did you make a plan to be nearby there yesterday?"

Now, Nick looked shamefaced. "I wanted to. I would have made a plan. I did know she was going to be there. But I couldn't because I had to be at work. I work long shifts, three days a week. Well into the evening. It's why I want to make a change, move into a different field."

"What work do you do?" Connor asked.

"I'm doing cab driving and transportation part-time."

"And were you busy in the afternoon, the day before yesterday, when Leanne was out on the trails?"

"Yes, I was. I was doing transportation for a function that took place downtown."

“What did that involve?”

“When the people finished at the function, they all had to be taken back to their hotels. So, I was driving nonstop from two p.m. through to about nine p.m. I can show you the route because it's mapped out on my GPS and dashcam. It was boring. Go to the venue, wait, pick up guests, take them to their hotel, and come straight back. I had to check in at each point with my GPS location. They insisted on that, or I didn’t get paid."

"Where's your phone?"

He glanced at a bag near one of the deck chairs. "It's in there."

"Let's have a look. Open it up for me."

He undid Nick's handcuffs and watched the man closely as he got up, gripping the towel, walked to the bag, and rummaged through it, producing an old-looking phone, which he opened.

"That's where I was," Nick pointed. "I can show you the route I took, the streets I drove. I can show you the time I picked up and dropped off the last of the guests. Then I signed off. It's all here." He swiped the screen and pointed again.

Cami was longing to know if there was any incriminating evidence on that phone, but the question didn't arise, because when Connor checked the mapping log and his cab bookings, he gave a reluctant nod.

Cami knew this meant he was not in the area when Leanne was killed. Since it was a serial, with those blue silicone bracelets left at the scenes, this meant he was cleared. She felt a thud of disappointment. She'd been so sure this was their man.

"You can go," Connor told him. "And stay out of trouble, you hear? Next time a cop or an FBI agent wants to speak to you, the smart thing to do is to cooperate."

He sounded annoyed, and Cami could see why, as Nick hurried off, looking relieved. Now, Connor was soaked to the skin. But luckily, if she knew her boss, he'd have a full change of clothes in the car.

"I'm going to get my bag," Connor said, confirming Cami's theory. "Wait here."

Connor stomped, or rather squelched, in the direction of the car. As soon as he'd left, his phone, which he'd left by the side of the pool with his gun belt, began ringing.

She edged over and took a look at the screen.

It was the office number on the line. She recognized it. That must mean Ethan was calling, and Cami wished she could pick up and speak to him. But answering her boss's call would be out of line.

The phone stopped and then restarted again.

Was this urgent? Cami had the feeling that it was. Ethan wouldn't be trying to call again and again unless something serious had happened.

Cami got her own phone out and dialed the office.

In a few rings, Ethan answered. He sounded stressed.

"I saw you were trying to get hold of Connor," she said. "He's getting changed into dry clothes after chasing a suspect. Is there a problem?"

"Yes, there is. There's been another murder," Ethan said, and Cami gripped her phone tighter, feeling horrified.

"Same MO," Ethan explained. "Same signature left at the scene. The victim lives south of Milwaukee. She's just been found, drowned in her own bathroom."

CHAPTER TEN

As Connor approached the crime scene, he saw it was already swarming with cops, as well as concerned bystanders. He parked the car and got out, feeling frustrated and worried that this killer was clearly on a spree. He—Connor was guessing it was a man, though not ruling out a strong woman—was making these kills at a rate that seemed far swifter than the average serial murderer.

It was almost as if he was on a specific mission. This felt like a rampage of death. That was how the angry mayor had referred to it.

"The FBI had better stop this rampage of death!" he'd said. "Our tax dollars aren't going to be wasted on incompetence and delays!"

And that had been before this latest victim had been found. He could only imagine what the mayor was saying now.

Distressing and devastating as another murder scene was, Connor hoped this one would provide more clues, because so far, there had been a worrying lack of them. Cami had realized that the victims were advertising their locations on social media, but it wasn't as if they weren't alone in that.

It sometimes seemed to Connor that everyone, apart from himself and a few others, was living their life firmly in the social spotlight. He acknowledged how dangerous it was. Connor didn't have children himself, but he had nieces and nephews whom he was constantly advising to be cautious. To think about what they put online. To not tell the world where they were going.

It only took one wrong person to follow you.

And this proved it.

"Let's take a look at the scene," he said, climbing out of the car, feeling heavy hearted as he always did when approaching the scene of a murder. A life had been taken, and Connor couldn't help feeling in his heart that he'd failed. That he should have been faster, should have somehow prevented this death.

One of the cops at the scene saw him approaching and hurried over, calling out, "FBI's here."

"I'm Detective Davies," the cop said.

"Agent Connor. This is IT expert Cami Lark."

Connor was used to the curious stares that Cami attracted with her edgy hairstyle—even though it was camouflaged by an FBI baseball cap—and her tattoos, even though they were mostly invisible under the jacket. Her multiple earrings in both ears were on display. It was only now that he saw her fingernails were painted black. To his surprise, Connor found he'd stopped noticing these physical details. It was as if his eyes passed over them, even though they'd annoyed him intensely on the first case he had handled with her.

Connor strode over the tidy lawn to the open front door of the house.

"The killer broke in. In broad daylight," the cop explained. "A passing neighbor was coming home from the shops, and saw the door standing ajar, and realized that the lock had been smashed. They went in, took one look, and called us."

That was interesting, Connor thought. Even though he knew Cami would be more focused on the online world, he was intrigued by that behavior. Because it did not signal clear planning. Rather, it was an impulsive, almost reckless crime. This killer could have broken in at night and killed this victim with far less risk of being discovered.

But he hadn't. He'd smashed the door and stormed the house in the late morning. That was hugely risky. And it indicated that they were dealing with a killer who was—in Connor's mind at least—probably not an organized or rational killer.

The smashed lock spoke of desperation, of seizing the moment. That was the mindset he sensed here.

He trod inside, through the small hall where he stopped to put on head and foot covers. In a scene like this, where the killer had acted frantically, there was far more chance that he'd made a mistake and perhaps left some trace behind. Maybe they'd been lucky.

"What's the victim's name?" he asked, knowing that Cami would be at the ready, researching it.

"Marion Albert," the detective replied. "She's forty years old."

Sure enough, Cami was already researching the victim.

"I've gotten into one of her online social media platforms. It looks like she sells homemade chocolates and cookies from home," Cami said. "Before she came home, she was at the planetarium. Not viewing the show. She was making deliveries to a kiosk there. She pinned her location there and then came back, probably just over an hour ago."

Someone had known, without a doubt, that she was coming home, Connor thought.

"And she's blonde," Cami said, hanging back as they approached the master bedroom where Connor guessed the drowning had occurred in the ensuite bathroom.

Another blonde. Was it a coincidence? Or was the killer seeking out women with this hair color for a reason?

Perhaps viewing the body would give him an insight, although as he stepped into the bathroom, he saw Cami hang back. She was not comfortable with seeing the crime scene and as always, Connor felt a flash of irritation because the crime scene was exactly where he needed the eyes, ears, and impressions of his partner.

The victim was floating in the bath, face down. Her fair hair fanned out around her head. There was a trace of blood in the chilly water, and Connor guessed that the killer had hit her over the head in the same way he'd killed the others, before dumping her in the bath to make sure she drowned. Since she was fully clothed, she hadn't been in the bath at the time. She must have been moved there, dragged or carried.

That indicated some strength, because she was a well-built woman, not petite. Again, Connor felt the parameters in his mind shift. Someone strong. Someone with the power and physical strength to move these victims.

There was the blue bracelet with the same red stud earring in place, set carefully on the side of the tub.

"There's no footprints, no trace of him to be found so far," the detective said. "We can't find any fingerprints so far, but we're continuing to look. The only ones on the scene appear to be the victim's."

The coroner was already on the scene, crouched over the tub, carefully examining the victim before draining the water.

"She's been dead about an hour, I'd guess," he said, turning to Connor. "Taking into account the temperature of the water which would have cooled her faster. This is very recent."

Connor bit his lip. Recent was still not good enough. An hour sounded like a short time, but in an hour, the killer could have escaped the city completely.

One of the cops carefully lifted the bracelet and placed it in an evidence bag. Connor hoped forensics could get something from it, but there had been nothing found on the others, he recalled.

From the other room, he heard Cami calling out, "Connor, can you come here real quick?"

Connor knew that she should come to him but wouldn't because of her dislike of murder scenes. As right now didn't seem like a good time to push that particular argument forward, Connor walked out. But then he saw what she had seen.

The victim's purse was hanging over a chair in the bedroom. And in the purse, Connor could see the shape of a phone.

"I might be able to find something on there," Cami told him, her face earnest. "It looks to be an older phone and a type I can unlock easily. Do you want me to take a look?"

Connor knew this was where the powers of his unusual partner could come into play. Her abilities would give him the chance to get ahead.

"Take a look," he said, after checking that she had gloves on and would not contaminate any evidence. The phone would need to be signed in and form part of the scene's evidence, so unless there was a compelling reason to sign it out again, what Cami found here—if anything—would be their only clue.

He turned back to the bathroom, glancing around him as he searched for any sign of where this might have happened. Where had she been attacked? He guessed it was very possible that, having been confronted by an intruder wielding some form of weapon, she'd fled. There was nothing visible on scene, so he must have brought it with him. Perhaps in terror, she'd run into the bathroom, and he'd attacked her and delivered the killing blow there. That would have made it easy for him.

But why her? That was what was puzzling Connor. What had made this killer target her?

And then, from the bedroom, he heard Cami call out again, this time sounding excited.

"I've got something!"

"You have?"

Quickly, Connor rushed through, to see what secrets the phone had yielded.

CHAPTER ELEVEN

Cami glanced up as Connor hurried back into Marion Albert's bedroom. She had been perched on the bed but quickly got up, not sure if sitting on a bed counted as contaminating the scene.

"This phone." She held it up in her gloved hand. "It's got malware on it. I've just found it running in the background."

Malware, thanks to her recent escapades in the FBI database, was something she was on the lookout for. It might be her own guilty secret, but perhaps it could help them on this case.

"What type of malware?" he asked.

"It's originating from a phishing scam, and it seems to have been used to collect personal information." She pressed more keys, keenly scrutinizing the program she'd just unearthed.

"You think that might be how he's targeted them?" Connor asked her. "Because that's what I've been wondering. Why them? There's nothing in common between them, besides that they are all blonde, which might be coincidental, and they all advertised their locations."

"I'm sure the fact that they advertised their locations is not a coincidence, and it's how he's tracking them, but I've also been asking myself how he's been finding them. Perhaps he put this onto social media and followed the people who downloaded it."

"And how would he have done that?" Connor asked. He sounded genuinely interested and Cami was surprised by how engaged he was over the process.

Was this really the same agent who'd seemed to shut down when anything IT-related was mentioned? She felt glad that he was becoming more interested in the world that she was so passionate about.

"In a quiz, it looks like," Cami said. "Online quizzes are the worst for that."

"They are?"

"They're information gathering in every way. If it's not trying to get passwords, it's harvesting personal details that can often be narrowed down by the quiz responses and even used to hack other confidential portals. There's risk in the quiz itself and in associated malware that tags along. My lecturer always says that when he advises younger people on how to stay safe online, and companies on their company policies, doing quizzes is one of the big no-nos, because people do them innocently and they think it's just fun. It's not like messaging a stranger or advertising where you're going—as these victims also did."

"Did the others do quizzes too?"

That was a good question. Turning to her own phone, Cami checked back on Patti's and Leanne's activities online.

"Yes, they did. Both of them did quizzes often. And all types too. Totally random ones."

She shook her head in disapproval. “Is there really a need to find out what type of car you would drive if you were a millionaire, or who your ideal celebrity boyfriend is, or what type of thunderstorm you are?” she asked.

“What type of storm? Seriously?” Connor's voice sounded like he thought some people had way too much time on their hands.

"I'm an electrical storm, powerful and dangerous. My lightning bolts will scorch you, and you can expect third degree burns if you get caught in my epicenter. Stay on my good side, and I'll bring you a shower of refreshing rain," Cami read aloud in disbelief.

"People do that?" Connor made a face. "Assuming, obviously, the answer is 'yes,' how can we track where this originated? I always thought that these types of quizzes originated in Eastern Europe for some reason."

"A lot of hacking activity does come from that region," Cami agreed, digging deeper into the quiz's code. "But it looks as if this particular malware is local. It's been launched from an IP address near here."

She turned to her mapping software to see if it would be possible to map the IP. Given that they'd had issues narrowing down IP addresses in the past, Cami had since gone hunting on the dark web and had found a few helpful programs that could pinpoint the origins of the IPs with more accuracy.

"I'm going to see if I can find it using this quick fix," she explained, glancing up at Connor.

His fascination with the online world had ebbed, and now he just looked impatient. "We need to get it fast," he urged.

"I'm doing my best," Cami said.

Her program was working, using information available in the public domain and networking it with other online activity. And as she watched, it got them a result.

"It looks like it's a cafe on the waterfront, near the starting point of one of the Milwaukee River cruises. Sam's Cafe, it's called."

"And how do we locate this person?"

"Well, the first step is to go there."

Connor wasted no more time. He turned to the door, and to Cami's relief, said, "Let's head straight to the cafe. I think we've gotten what we needed from this scene."

***

Sam's Cafe was a big, popular place, overlooking the Milwaukee River, with about thirty tables inside and another ten or so outside on the boardwalk beyond the entrance.

The staff were dressed in navy blue shirts with white piping, in homage to its waterfront location perhaps, and the walls were filled with local art. At this hour, with lunch under way, almost every table was taken.

“Can you tell where he is?”

“I need some time to pinpoint it,” Cami said cagily. This wasn’t as simple as Connor seemed to think it would be. She hoped that he wouldn’t get mad at her when he found that out.

"Let's go stand at the bar," Connor decided. He wove his way to the bar that lined the right side of the cafe and stood in the corner with his back to the wall, surveying the room.

He'd left the only seat for Cami, and she took it, hitching herself onto it and looking around, taking in the bustle and buzz of this busy cafe.

With so many people here, Cami hoped there was a high likelihood that the hacker who'd written this program would be here, looking to send it out and trap more unwary users in his information-sucking web. But he wasn’t here yet, to her unease.

"Now, how do we find him?" Connor asked.

Cami stared at him, feeling worried. He was still looking very impatient, and she didn't think he was going to like her answer.

"We wait," she said.

Sure enough, his eyebrows shot up. "Wait?" he asked incredulously.

"I've got some software running that will tell us as soon as he connects up here. And he has often connected at lunch time in the past."

"You mean he's not here? And this is the only way of finding him?"

"Yes."

"We could be waiting here all week!" he spluttered. "How often does he come in?"

"He's been here three times in the past week," she said placatingly. She didn't think her tone would work, though, and sure enough, Connor seethed.

"That's less than fifty percent of the time!"

"I'm not sure how else to do it," Cami admitted. "He's not going to come to us, and we don't know where he lives, or how to get hold of him, or even who he is. This is the only way to find him. He was last here two days ago, so hopefully he's due a visit today, and he'll soon be sitting here, trying to send out the malware to more people."

"We give it an hour," Connor decided.

"An hour should do it. He often seems to connect at lunch time. I guess that's because it's busy, probably so he can target the most people online, and also because it's more difficult for him to be noticed."

Connor checked his watch, then looked around the room. Cami saw him look at his watch again, and she knew he was counting down the time. Most definitely, on the hour, he was going to say they must leave.

Where was this man, this invisible hacker? She was sure that he was going to sign in today. He'd never had more than a two-day gap in the past. She knew that Connor still didn't entirely trust the process she used to get this information. She wanted to earn his trust and that made it all the more urgent that her hunch paid off.

She stared down, willing him to sign in, willing her program to alert her to his whereabouts.

Just as she was on the point of giving up, it happened.

The code lit up. There was activity online, and that meant he was using the secret program.

"He's here," she said, feeling her heart speed up. "I can see his code. I can see it's linked to a username. Landon Graham. That must be him, and he's just logged in."

"Where?"

"That's what we have to look for. He will have just arrived."

"I've been keeping track," Connor said. "There are only two people who've sat down in the last five minutes. Both have been on their own. One was over to the right, an older woman who looks to be waiting for someone. And the other is straight ahead."

He pointed to a studious-looking man in his twenties, who was staring intently at a large laptop.

"It's him," Cami said with a nod. It could be nobody else.

Time to ask some questions and to get answers from this mystery hacker.

Cami rushed over to the hacker, shoulder to shoulder with Connor, feeling her pulse race at the thought of the confrontation ahead. He looked like a normal type of guy. Studious, with spectacles and suspenders over a white, well ironed shirt. He looked preppy and ordinary and nowhere close to the mental image that Cami was sure most people had of what a hacker would be like.

He looked up in surprise as they sat down opposite him. He was clearly in his own little world, oblivious to the people around him. But as his eyes widened, Cami saw that he was quickly realizing who they were and that their arrival spelled trouble.

"FBI," Connor said. “We need to speak to you.”

The man acted instantly, and surprisingly fast.

He shoved the table toward them violently, so that its edge hit Cami in the stomach, and she let out a choking gasp.

And then, having grabbed his laptop with lightning speed, he was out. A chair clattered down as he pushed it aside.

Landon Graham was on the run, fleeing the cafe. He'd gotten the jump on them, he'd seized the element of surprise, and now they were at risk of him getting away.

CHAPTER TWELVE

Connor shoved the table away, so hard that the salt and pepper cellars teetered and wobbled and then clattered down. And the next moment, in a rush, he was out.

Feeling breathless with shock, Cami scrambled to her feet and hurtled out of the cafe after him.

She couldn't believe this. In front of their eyes, Landon Graham had taken flight and was now racing down a side road that seemed to lead to a recycling center. On the blacktopped surface, several large containers of various colors stood. Landon wove his way in between two of them and abruptly disappeared from sight.

Connor swore under his breath as he powered down the hill and into the center, taking the same route their suspect had gone.

"FBI! Stop!" he yelled, but Landon took no notice, and if anything, his headlong flight accelerated. *He must know the area,* Cami thought. He must have found a side entrance and be speeding out already, because Connor was darting the same way and was now visible in the alley beyond the center.

Connor had pulled ahead of her and that wasn't helpful at all. She was already losing him, seeing the two men race further and further away.

She sped up, trying to accelerate. She could feel her lungs burning, her legs aching, and she forced herself to go faster.

She had no idea what she was doing, she was just blindly following Connor. But she wanted to be there for him. She wanted to support him. She wanted to be there to back him up.

She wanted to be his equal.

But she knew she wasn't. He was a trained FBI agent, and she wasn't trained for this. She hadn't been co-opted onto the FBI for her running ability. She'd been forced to help them because of her coding and hacking prowess.

And yet, she was still running. She was still going to pursue this man with everything she had, and she would help to take him down, if she possibly could. As she saw him turn a corner and disappear, she surged on. She raced down the alley, hurtling over a trash can and skimming a low wall behind the two men, with speed and agility that surprised her.

Now, they were racing down the alleyway, and as she entered it, they exited, turning hard right.

Cami's shoes were feeling like lead weights at the end of her feet. She felt as if she was bursting with the effort.

She wasn't going to give up. Not now. Not when she needed to keep Connor and the fleeing suspect in sight. Not when she could feel it, the close presence of danger, the adrenaline racing through her veins.

She'd left the cafe far behind her. There was nothing now, besides the quick pounding of her own frantic running and the thumping of her heart in her ears. She wasn't going to give up. She was going to run as fast as she could and do everything she could to help them catch this guy.

And then, suddenly, the alleyway opened into a large, open space. It was a parking area, and she could see Connor and Landon racing between the rows of cars.

More running! How had Connor done this? How did he do this every day? Nothing had prepared her for this. She wasn't a runner. She loved to walk. But she'd been hired for her smarts, not her fitness. Just as well, because fitness had failed her totally now. She wasn't able to run another step. All the resolve in the world was not going to change basic physiology and the fact that she was past her own limits.

What else could she do. Feeling defeated, Cami stopped, leaning against the fence and gasping for air.

Was there any other way she could get to him? She had some basic information on him. Could she get more? Could she find anything else from this underhanded hacker, this creator of malware, who'd fled when the FBI had arrived?

He had his phone and laptop with him. He'd logged into the cafe when he gotten there. She'd had programs running then, to pick him up, and they might still be running now. She might be able to see his access logs. Maybe there would be more information on them, or something that could help her.

She was so exhausted and starved of air that her hands were shaking as she accessed the information.

It was partially downloaded, not fully. She didn't have everything she needed. What did she have?

Aha. Here was something. She had an online app payment. He'd booked his wifi immediately on arrival. And from that, Cami realized, she could see his home address.

Gasping for breath, she checked it out on her maps app. Her mind was racing with possibilities. Chief among them was whether Landon had been trying to lose the FBI so that he could bolt for home and lock himself away.

"Okay. It's not too far. He could have gone there. Or be taking a roundabout route," she concluded.

Interestingly, it was a ten-minute walk from the cafe. He lived in an apartment block just three streets down. He hadn't gone straight there. But that had been because he'd fled in a panic and was hoping to lose Connor in this twisting, turning route he'd taken. If she'd been him, she'd have headed home.

She'd now completely lost both Landon and Connor. So, she had a choice. It was go back to the cafe, or head to his house.

Going back to the café was pointless because he wouldn't be there. There was no way he would have headed back there again.

Cami checked the maps once more, fixing the route to his place into her mind. And then at a fast walk, because she didn't trust her legs not to buckle under her if she tried to run again, she set off for the apartments. They were only a block away from where she was now, a surprisingly short distance.

The apartment buildings were set back from the road, an enclave of two- and three-story buildings that formed a mini estate. She walked up to it, seeing the main entrance ahead. He was on the ground floor of apartment three.

There didn't seem to be any security in place at the main gate, and she guessed each apartment had its own bell or buzzer. She felt her throat tighten.

What if he was there? What if he was in his house right now, packing his bags and readying to run? She'd have to face him alone if Connor had lost him.

What if he was nowhere around, and she'd made a huge mistake? That was an even worse eventuality.

But for now, she should send Connor the coordinates. He might be running, but if he wasn't, he might need them. Quickly, Cami messaged them to him with the words, *"Landon's address."*

She took a deep breath. She felt a little calmer now, and she felt ready to walk into the face of danger.

Apartment three was set one back from the road. She followed the paved path around to it and found the door for his unit.

It was locked up tight. The blinds were drawn, and she couldn't hear anything from inside.

Cami hesitated. Should she wait here? Or should she go back to the main road and keep a lookout for Connor, either arriving or messaging her back.

But, at that moment, there was a thump of footsteps and her head jerked up.

Landon, looking frantic and exhausted, with his laptop bag bouncing on his back, sprinted along the walkway. He had his key in his hand, ready to unlock the door. When he saw Cami, he stopped dead, an expression of shock on his face.

He turned and began sprinting the other way.

"No! Wait!"

Feeling appalled that this chase was starting all over again and that Connor was nowhere to be seen, Cami forced her aching legs to move and set off in pursuit.

CHAPTER THIRTEEN

Cami raced after Landon, feeling shocked that this was happening all over again. Shocked and worried, because now it was up to her to chase him down. At least she could see that the zigzag route, which must have succeeded in losing Connor, had also taken its toll on him. His limbs were flailing. He was puffing for breath, stumbling over the curbside as he reached the pedestrian path.

And there, to her extreme relief, she saw Connor racing in his direction. Sending the coordinates had been the right thing to do. The cavalry had arrived, and now there was nowhere for Landon to go.

Again, he hesitated and turned, but that only meant he was facing Cami, and the next moment, Connor grabbed his arm from behind.

"Enough, now," he said, puffing out the words to the exhausted suspect. "Enough now. You're coming in for questioning. I'm going to call a car to fetch you now. And don't try anything else."

To make sure he didn't, Connor handcuffed his hands behind him before making the call. Just a couple of minutes later, a police car pulled up.

"We'll take him in, and give you a ride back to your car," the officer at the wheel said.

Cami had never been so relieved to collapse on the comfortable fabric of the car's passenger seat. Her legs were aching, and she spent the short ride to Connor's car trying to get her breath back and her thoughts in order to prepare for the questioning ahead. Luckily, Landon seemed to be just as sapped from the run. He spent the journey in silence and didn't struggle or complain at all.

They changed cars when they reached the place where Connor had parked and drove behind the other cops to the local police department. Once at the local police department, they unloaded Landon and escorted him in. Connor took him straight to the front desk.

"We have a suspect to question. Is there an interview room available?"

Cami was getting used to the look and feel of these rooms, which the police officer showed them to as soon as Landon had been officially signed in and his details taken. She was used to the bright lighting, the featureless walls, and the observation window, which she knew was made of one-way glass.

They all sat down. Landon was out of handcuffs. He was fidgeting, looking deeply uneasy, with his shoulders hunched. He wasn't making eye contact with either her or Connor, Cami saw.

"You know why we came to speak to you?" Connor asked.

Landon shook his head.

"It was because we tracked malware back to your IP address. You've been sending it out, gathering people's information. Correct?"

Landon swallowed hard. Finally, in a hoarse voice, he started to talk. "I'm sorry, I don't know what you mean. You seem to think I'm some kind of a criminal? I'm not."

"Malware on its own is serious enough. But you've been embedding it in quizzes, and we have three recent murder victims who did those quizzes. Was this how you tracked them?" Connor asked harshly.

"Look, I don't know what you're talking about." He was breathing almost as hard as he had done when running, Cami saw.

"We've been following your online activities for a while, and we've seen what you've been doing," Connor insisted.

"This is some kind of mistake, right? It isn't me. I don't do that kind of stuff."

Connor leaned forward over the table, his face hard. "Don't be a fool, Landon. My colleague here is an IT expert. She can get the information off your computer, probably faster than you can blink. So, you might as well admit to it before she goes looking."

Now, Landon's gaze swung to Cami, and he stared at her, looking appalled.

"No, no, no," he said, appearing to panic. "I don't know what you think I'm doing, but you got the wrong guy. You got the wrong guy."

"Let me see your computer then," she challenged him. "It's been signed in with the rest of your possessions. We can sign it out again and take a look inside."

Cami saw Landon's eyes widen in horror. He clearly believed her.

"Don't you dare," he said. Cami was shocked by his vehemence.

"You won't have a choice. As a suspect, we're now entitled to investigate related evidence," Connor explained.

"I never killed anyone!" Landon's voice was now high and stressed. He looked as frantic as if he'd suddenly landed in a nightmare.

"You'll need to prove that in a court of law if you don't agree to speak to us and give us answers," Connor threatened.

"Please, I haven't done anything wrong—well, not more than just an innocent piece of software. I'm not a murderer." Landon now sounded as if he was begging to be believed.

It was surprising how much younger he looked now, Cami thought. Younger and more scared. He was out of his depth here, that was for sure.

"We know that you've been sending out malware to people," Connor continued, "and we know that you've been using it to access other people's computers, to find out about their personal information."

"I—it was just some fun," Landon whispered. “To see if I could.”

"That's highly illegal. Especially when it's done in order to commit a murder."

"I'm not a killer. Okay, look, I admit—I did run the malware. I was just checking to see if the program worked, that was all. I never intended to commit any crime with the information. I was going to destroy it. Honestly."

If there was one thing Cami was learning from her time in the FBI, it was that people who said ‘honestly’ were usually not being honest at all.

"You need to tell us your whereabouts this morning. And yesterday evening, and the previous evening also," Connor said firmly. "If you don't have an alibi for the times of these murders, then you're a suspect. That's a fact, and nothing is going to change it."

"I can show you where I was. What will you accept? My phone has a record of the GPS routes I've taken. I'm a delivery driver part-time for a courier company, and I was working yesterday evening. I'll show you where. I don't have an alibi for this morning because I was at home. But for last night, I do. I’ll show you if you give me my phone back.”

Connor stepped outside the interview room. A minute later, he was back with the phone.

With shaking hands, Landon navigated to his phone and pulled up the GPS coordinates.

"You see, when I get a delivery, I map it and then I go there. That's what I did the whole of yesterday. I started at seven a.m., and I only signed off at seven p.m. That's what I was doing. I swear, I wasn't killing people. I wouldn't do that. I also did some deliveries the previous afternoon.”

"The malware is a crime on its own. And you're going to be charged for it," Connor told him harshly. "People deserve for their personal information to be kept private, and not have individuals mining it and selling it. So, the police here are going to be dealing with that." He sighed. "However, I see that you do have your time accounted for last night and the previous afternoon also. You could not have been committing the murder at the aquarium, or the murder out on the hiking trails."

Cami let out a disappointed breath.

This hacker was not their killer. But as he'd been speaking, as Connor had listed those locations all over again, Cami felt as if the pin drops had created a pattern in her mind.

A pattern.

Quickly referring to her laptop, sitting in the interview room while Connor led the hacker out to the main police station, Cami checked to see if her hunch might be accurate.

Here was where the first murder had occurred, on the trails north of the city. The second had occurred near the city center, at the aquarium. And the third had taken place south of the city.

It was as if the killer was moving swiftly, in a southerly direction, through Milwaukee and on a route that would eventually take him to Chicago. Without a doubt, there was a pattern here.

But Cami had no idea what it meant. Was this killer en route somewhere and choosing victims as he went? Or was he plotting a path based on his victims' locations?

She didn't know that, but based on the map, she had a good idea where he might strike again.

It would be ten or twenty miles further south, if her guess was right, out in the countryside beyond Milwaukee.

Was there any way we can prevent another death? Cami wondered, feeling that for the first time, they might be catching up.

CHAPTER FOURTEEN

The stars were calling to the lost man, and now he felt sure that he knew which way he was supposed to go. He had the route fixed in his mind. Finally, he had guidance once more.

"This is it, what I need. I can reach it this way. Find them," he muttered as a picture of them flashed briefly into his mind.

"But what if you can't?" the devil that always seemed to sit on his shoulder asked.

"I will," he insisted, fighting this unwelcome voice. "If I get it wrong, I know what I need to do. I've done it before, and I will do it again. Every mistake gets me closer."

He didn't want to think about those mistakes again, the violence inherent in those moments, the way he felt as he did what he needed to do. At the time, it was strangely satisfying and even felt addictive. But afterward, he felt regret, and tried to convince himself that he took no joy in what he'd done. They were mistakes, and they needed to be fixed in order to make things right again. That was all.

Once he'd killed all the imposters, all the lookalikes, then the people he was seeking would remain. That was his logic, and he knew that he could rely on it.

The moonlight shone down on him, its silvery glow illuminating the landscape. It was so bright that the lost man could see his path clearly now. His body was aching, his legs were protesting, and his mind was darkening, but he needed to keep going.

It had been a long time since he'd been outside of the city limits. He had no idea what to expect from the country. The sky seemed to stretch out endlessly above him. It felt like he could reach out and touch the vastness of space.

Strangely, the world felt easier to navigate as well. He knew where he was going, and he was able to drive toward that goal.

It was a long drive, but it didn't take him as long as he'd anticipated, as he thought he knew exactly where he was going. He hoped so, at least.

He had his route clear now. He knew the way forward, even though it was through what felt like the unknown. But it was not unknown, of course. It was all too familiar.

"You should stop this," the voice in his head told him as he drove along, his headlights bright in the dark, glancing up at the stars every so often before returning his veering course to the road.

"I'm not going to stop it," he insisted.

"You're never going to find what you need," the voice told him, and there was a confidence there he didn't like.

"You're just following what you think you know. You're lost, and every step you take is getting you further from where you need to be."

But the lost man knew that that was the point. He had to find what he was looking for, no matter what it took. He had to find it. Ever since the memories had surged into his mind, and he'd realized how badly he'd strayed from his place in the world, he'd known this had to be done.

He knew how this story would end. He just needed to get there.

"I'm not lost," he insisted, shaking his head as he held his phone and his GPS. He was certain that this route was correct. He was certain that he would find what he needed to fix his mistakes.

But the voice in his head wouldn't stop tormenting him. "At this rate, you're going to do what you've done before. You're going to see everything destroyed again. Do you want to see that once more? Are you ready for it? And once you've done that, what are you going to do? What is the point of all this?"

"Don't torment me that way."

"It's true, though? Now that you know what you did, you remember?"

He couldn't answer that. He didn't know how to answer that.

And then as the voice in his head started to laugh, he slammed his hands against the steering wheel in frustration.

"Shut up!" he shouted aloud.

He'd never felt so bad in his entire life. His muscles were trembling, his body was on high alert, and his mind was so dark, he was sure that he could never come back from this place of despair.

But there was always hope. There must be. He just needed to be strong enough to see it through.

"Why do you want to destroy things all over again?" the voice insisted, but the lost man was already past the point of listening.

He didn't care whether he survived this anymore. He didn't care if he lost himself. Right now, there was no hope of finding the happy ending that he needed. That was the point of all this, after all. If he didn't keep searching, he would never, ever find it.

There, ahead. That was where the stars were leading him. He was close. He might even be close enough to see them again.

He felt a surge of excitement.

He was going to save them. He was going to save them this time. He was going to make his life worth something. He was going to repair the mistakes that had happened, that had sent his life spinning off into chaos, that had caused the memories to be obliterated for long, empty years.

He was utterly sure it could be done.

This farmhouse ahead. That was the place he needed. That lone building, with its twinkling lights, aligned perfectly with the signal he'd been following, and it was in the right direction too. This was it, and he knew that she was here, waiting.

Aunt Barbie. That was who was here. He'd seen her online and hoped it was her.

He killed the lights. He wasn't sure why he did that and put it down to sheer instinct, nothing more. But he knew that it was essential to approach in the dark, although he couldn't remember why. It was something to do with not being found. That was it. He needed not to be found, because if he was, his mission would be destroyed.

He eased off on the accelerator, coasting in, trying his best to keep his fractured mind on the job, because it felt as if it was veering in a thousand different directions.

This was the only thing he had left in his life, the only hope that remained.

He eased the car to a stop, making sure to do it so carefully that not a sound could be heard. There were other sounds in the night. The calling of birds from somewhere. The sleepy clucking of chickens. The faraway rush of a car along the road he'd recently left. He saw its headlights pass by, like a distant meteor, and watched it until it had gone. If it turned this way, it would mean trouble, and his heart thudded hard in his chest.

But the car continued along the main road and then things grew quiet again.

He turned back to the house and stared at it, looking at the stars wheeling overhead. They had brought him to the right place, they must surely have done.

Here, he knew he would find what he needed. He felt confident. The stars had shown him the way, and it had to be. It had to be. In this small cottage, he would find his goal, his wish, his dream. At last.

Before he walked to the house, he reached into the car and took out his stick. Just as a precaution. He was sure he wouldn't need it. But it felt good in his hand. That was all.

On the way to the front door, something caught his eye.

A reservoir of water located near the house.

Its darkly gleaming surface seemed to reflect the stars, and the lost man paused for a moment, watching the hypnotic ripples, and touching the bracelet in his pocket, before striding up to the door.

CHAPTER FIFTEEN

"Surely we can do something. There must be something we could do now?" Cami said, standing in the lobby of the motel where she and Connor had just arrived and were staying overnight.

Connor nodded. "The kills do form a geographical pattern," he said in a low voice, so that the receptionist behind the counter didn't hear him speak. "You're absolutely right about that. But we can't get anywhere with it. It's too vague. It heads in a southerly direction, correct. It seems like this killer is heading toward Chicago. But the gaps in between the murder sites vary. We can't look at that map and say: in fifteen miles exactly, he's going to kill again."

Cami felt her stomach churning. "I know. But there must be action we can take?" She stared at him angrily. Was he refusing to hear her again? Was this what this was about? Were they going to have another fight?

She saw him frown back and she felt ready. Ready for the fight. Even though she wasn't sure what she could do.

But it seemed Connor was on her side after all. "There are a few options open to us. Apart from physically being there to prevent another kill, which is impossible, there's plenty we can do. So let's go into the meeting room and get it done."

Cami headed up the stairs behind him, holding her room key tightly. She felt exhausted to the bone. Going through such a long day on two hours of sleep had left her feeling shattered. But at the same time, she wasn't ready to quit. And she didn't feel like it was right to sleep.

The killer was out there, speeding through the night, cutting through the map coordinates like a blade as he headed to . . . to what? That was what she didn't know.

They walked into the small meeting room that Connor had booked for an hour, because this motel was beds only, small and basic, no workspace available in the bedrooms.

The blinds in the meeting room were still open. She gazed out at the parking lot, seeing the lights of the cars, the beams swinging around as they departed. She stared into the darkness where she knew the killer was.

Connor strode over and closed the blinds. He sat at the small wooden table and opened his laptop. Then he got on the phone.

"Ethan," he said.

"Here, boss. Just got back from a long day's stakeout and finished planning with the team. We'll be ready to do the traffickers' takedown tomorrow. What's happening there?" Ethan's voice, cheerful and sounding amazingly wide awake, made Cami feel better.

"We've identified a pattern to the killer. He seems to be working his way south. Based on this, we need to alert all police departments south of Milwaukee, and on the routes heading to Chicago."

"What are they on the lookout for?"

Connor sighed. "There hasn't been enough camera evidence to identify this guy's car. But undoubtedly, he has a car. So, most likely a single male, driving alone. He may have a weapon of some kind in the car with him. A stick, perhaps. They need to set up roadblocks and be on high alert. They need to be wary of men on their own traveling at night. So far, he seems to have targeted women on their own."

"Blonde women," Cami said.

Connor nodded. "Blonde women."

Ethan sighed. "That is something, but it doesn't give us a whole lot to go on."

"No, it doesn't. Acknowledged. But at least it's something. It's the most we can do."

"I'll get the word out," Ethan said, sounding resigned.

"There's something else," Cami said. Connor looked at her curiously.

"What is it?" he asked.

"Cameras," she said. "We had the camera footage from the aquarium's parking lot sent to us. I'm sure there were no cameras out on the hiking trails, but it's possible that there might be a camera somewhere close to the third victim's house? She lived in a suburb. Maybe a security camera, a traffic camera, something nearby?"

"Good idea," Connor approved. "Ethan, get the team to have a look and see if we can track down any cameras. If we can get two sets of camera footage, we can start to narrow down if the same car was in the right place at the right time."

That was great for the future. But what about now? Wasn't there more to be done? It didn't seem so, because Connor was wrapping up with Ethan, concluding the call.

Cami felt appalled that there wasn't more they could do, but at the same time, when she looked at the map, she saw the harsh reality of what they were up against. The area south of Milwaukee was huge. They were looking at a network of routes between two major cities. Yes, the killer was out there, without a doubt. Most likely he was heading south. But beyond that, the parameters were way too frustratingly broad to be able to pick anything else up.

"Get some sleep," Connor said, packing up his phone and laptop.

He'd stopped at a grocery store on the way to the motel and had bought some supplies. Sandwiches, chocolate bars, bottled water, and sodas, easy food to eat on the go. He'd divided it into two bags, and one of those he now pushed over to Cami.

"Have some food, and get some rest," he told her. "You look as if you're ready to pass out from tiredness. We start again at six a.m. Or earlier if the situation changes."

He didn't need to spell that out for her. It would be earlier if another murder was called in.

"Okay. See you at six."

There was no point in arguing further because she now accepted there was nothing they could do. Cami turned and headed out of the meeting room, walking up the stairs to her bedroom, which was a floor above.

She was getting used to the look and feel of these motel rooms. They were the same—basic but well equipped and strangely comforting in their anonymity.

When she'd showered and devoured two of the sandwiches and a soda while sitting on the small armchair, she got into bed. But her mind was too active to sleep. She texted Ethan, wondering if he was still up.

"You awake?"

"Yes. Back home, but awake. You turning in now?"

"I am. I'm thinking of this guy, this killer. I feel so helpless. He's going to kill again, and I haven't been able to use enough technology to find him."

"I know. But you can't help that. I'm sure you will."

"I feel like I'm not doing enough." Cami sighed as she keyed in the words.

"I know. But you're doing the best you can. He might make a mistake, do something that will give you a better picture. You can't do the impossible. I've learned that on cases."

"I guess so."

"Don't let yourself get too caught up in the what ifs. Get some rest. Tomorrow, you and me and Connor, we'll catch this guy."

"It's a deal."

Cami took a deep breath, feeling better, realizing that he was right. She couldn't control this situation. She was doing all she could. Cami put her phone on the bedside table and stared out of the window, seeing the gleam of the moon, and the strip of lights from the parking lot.

Not quite ready to give up for the day, she opened her phone again, looking at the meager case file that had been all the FBI had gathered on her sister. Did her family know more? Had her father given more information to the FBI, trusting that they would handle the case, and had they suppressed it or destroyed it for some reason?

She'd never thought that way before. She'd never had anything but angry thoughts about her father, her family, since that catastrophe had played out. It felt weird, now, to think of her father as not being the main villain in this tragedy. What if he'd been a victim in a way, unable to take this further because of the police protocol and the structures of law enforcement?

But why had that case not been more thoroughly investigated? Why so little information?

Was it just an incompetent agent, or was there more to it? After all, surely there was a reason why that file had had the malware added to it, ready to seek and destroy if anyone tried to access it?

She wondered again how much IT knowledge that agent had possessed, if he was the one who'd done this.

She put down her cell phone, then lay on her back on the bed, staring up at the ceiling. She felt emotionally drained. She lay there pondering this, thinking about the map, her eyes heavy, her mind unwilling to switch off.

She didn't think she would fall asleep, but she did, even though her rest was uneasy and punctuated by nightmares. In them, she was running along a long, dark corridor. She knew that Jenna was at the end. She was certain of it. But the way was blocked by a shadowy figure whose face she couldn't see. He had a menacing, aggressive presence, and he was not going to let her pass.

"Let me through!" she screamed at him. "Let me through. I need to find her!"

She began hammering him with her fists, trying to make him move away, hitting and punching him.

And suddenly, she was sitting bolt upright in bed, with gray light seeping through the blinds. The hammering was Connor, knocking on her door, calling out in a sharp, tense voice.

"Cami? We need to get going. There's been another murder just called in."

CHAPTER SIXTEEN

Cami felt a sick sensation in the pit of her stomach as she heard Connor's voice outside her door. Another murder. This killer was continuing his rampage. This was evil, pure and unadulterated. It was all the worse to have known that it was going to happen and to feel that she had somehow not been able to prevent it. Guilt churned inside her even though she knew it was irrational to feel this way.

"I'm coming," she called, her voice hoarse after her night of deep, though nightmare-infested, sleep. At least her mind felt sharper again.

Quickly, she pulled on her clothes and grabbed up her things. She hurried out of the room. Connor was there, looking grim. He was dressed in a black top and jeans, his gun in a holster on his belt, his FBI jacket slung over his shoulders. He did not look rested, and he was frowning, his face set in troubled lines.

"Let's go," he said.

"Where was the murder?" she asked, as they hustled downstairs and out to the car. The car clock showed it was five forty-five.

"On a small farm, a few miles south of Milwaukee, near the Interstate 94."

"And who's the victim?" Cami asked as Connor started up and drove out into the brightening morning.

"Her name is Sally-Anne Brewster," Connor said.

Feeling that this, at least, was something she could do now, Cami looked up the name.

"She also pinned her location regularly," she told Connor. "There doesn't seem to be a reason. She just seems to be someone who likes social media."

She was pretty, with a broad, open face and bright eyes. She had short, curly, blonde hair and she was smiling, happy. Cami felt a pang, knowing this woman was dead.

"If we could only have saved you, or caught him before he got to you," she whispered softly to herself, in apology and remorse.

Then, she read the brief bio that appeared next to the picture. Sally-Anne Brewster. Twenty-seven years old. Originally from Brooklyn, New York. She was living alone in a rented cottage on a small farm.

That, she knew, was where they were headed now, but she felt a sense of frustration that the killer would have left the scene hours ago.

"I know it feels like too little too late," Connor said as if reading her mind. "But there may be something to be found here. Something this scene can tell us."

Ahead, she could already see the flashing lights and the emergency vehicles pulling up to the scene. This was a typical small farm, with a wooden ranch house and some outbuildings, including the quaint cottage. The air smelled fresh. Cami's gaze was instantly drawn to the water reservoir near the buildings. There were police and emergency workers clustered around it.

That must be where she'd been drowned.

Climbing out of the car, she surveyed the scene, piecing together the clues. The front door of the cottage was splintered. It hadn't been a strong door, but a cheap and flimsy wooden one. Not that she thought a strong door would have kept him out. It seemed nothing could keep him out. But without a doubt, he'd known she was inside.

Connor strode over to the reservoir, and Cami trailed behind, knowing what she would see, reluctant to face the violent finality that showed where a woman's life had ended.

He'd broken into the cottage. He'd struck her over the head with his weapon like he did with the others. Then he'd taken her to the reservoir. Were there any footprints? Cami doubted it. She guessed the police had already scoured the gravel path for prints and found none.

Knowing him, he would have worn gloves, she guessed, because they'd found no visible trace evidence at these scenes so far.

However, the low, white-painted concrete wall of the reservoir was spattered with blood that she guessed belonged to the victim. Her head wound must have been bleeding as he dragged her to the water.

"It happened last night," a man wearing gloves and a mask said, looking up from the examination of the body. "But it's difficult to give an accurate time in these circumstances. Around eight to twelve hours ago would be my guess. But we may be able to confirm it better in the postmortem."

"Who found the body?" Connor asked.

"One of the farm workers, arriving in the morning. He saw the blood and went to look," one of the police officers said. "The farmer and his family are on vacation, so she was the only one on the property last night. Unfortunately, that means there were no eyes or ears around to pick anything up."

Had this killer known that, Cami wondered, *or had it just been a lucky coincidence?*

She stood back, watching as the police and the forensics team followed their procedures. A small crowd of neighbors had gathered at a distance, watching. She turned her head away as the body, streaming water, was lifted carefully out of the reservoir and placed on a waiting gurney. The armband had already been bagged.

She noticed the woman's blonde hair, looking darker because it was soaked from her long immersion.

They were all blondes. All the victims. This had to mean something! And they had all been dumped in water. Not just because the water was nearby, either. What Connor had said about scenes providing clues was true. This scene was showing her that the killer had had to walk a couple of hundred yards to get to that reservoir. It was not exactly convenient. Perhaps the tiny cottage hadn't had a bathtub, Cami guessed.

And this killer clearly had a compulsion to place his victims in water. Drowning was part of what he did.

Now, she needed to work out why. Why was he doing this? There was something about this scene, the way he had clearly carried this victim so far to dump her unconscious body in the water, that got Cami thinking.

This felt like a compulsion to her. He was being driven to do it. Blondes, water, drowning. Where was the link? Could she possibly find it?

Connor strode back toward her, his face grim.

"Connor, it's like he's compelled to dump them in water," Cami said, wanting to test out her theory.

"Like a ritual, maybe," Connor agreed. "Or else, he just wants to minimize the risk of trace evidence on the scene. So far, we've found no evidence of the murder weapon in the wounds. No splinters, no fragments. Could be due to the water."

"To me, it seems very intentional, very deliberate, but I wouldn't say it was to hide the evidence. He could have left her under the shower to do that, to wash out the wound. There seems to be something about water, about drowning, that's important to him."

"I agree," he said, finally acknowledging her point even though he'd tested it by arguing against it. "There's something about this that feels like it has significance to him."

"I wonder if we search online, whether we can find anything related to this," Cami said thoughtfully.

"Linked cases?"

"Yes, or even a traumatic event. Maybe—I don't know—maybe his blonde girlfriend drowned and that triggered him to start killing."

"Search." Connor spread his arms. "The more information we can find now, the better."

Cami turned to her phone.

Could she find some connection to the killer, some hint of why he was doing what he did, if she searched using the parameters she had in mind? Perhaps something would come up.

"I'll use apostrophe searches to narrow the parameters," she said thoughtfully.

Connor stared at her blankly for a moment. "Yes," he then said. "I'm sure you will."

There was a note of dark humor in his tone. It was a hundred times better than the angry criticism that had characterized so much of their first days together.

Using the key words "blonde," "drowning," "Chicago," and "Milwaukee," Cami began to search.

When the results came up, she narrowed them by news. She looked again, scanning the fields quickly. She didn't know exactly what she was looking for, but she guessed that it would check a few of the boxes, and that she would know more if she found it.

There had to be a reason why he was doing this, she told herself. Keep searching, keep searching. And then, her heart sped up as she found a result.

It wasn't just a result. This was significant. It was not a recent news report. It was about five years old, but it had very clear parallels to what they were dealing with.

"Connor!" she called, now feeling excited. "I've got something here."

CHAPTER SEVENTEEN

Cami and Connor crowded together in the car and Cami opened her laptop, calling up the news article on the bigger screen so that it would be easier to read. They needed details here because she was sure this article was gold.

"It's a family who died, driving off a bridge in winter," she said. "'Tragic Crash Claims the Becker Family,' it's headlined. The car slipped on ice when they were close to Chicago. The car went into a lake and all six occupants drowned."

She closed her eyes for a moment. That was a terrible tragedy, and there was something about it that chilled her blood. She could imagine what it must have been like to be in that car. To feel it start to slide on the ice. To have that terrible lurch of the stomach as the car lost control and went spinning off the road to land in the deep lake that looked icy and inhospitable.

"It must have been the scariest thing," she said. "Traumatic for everyone. And they all died? That's just terrible. I mean, it always seems that in these accidents, one person at least manages to survive."

"And I see that there was a big family in the car," Connor said, peering intently at the article.

Cami nodded. "The Becker family. There was a mother, two daughters, a son, a grandmother, and an aunt. The daughters were in their late teens. The son was twenty. And they're all blonde. Very blonde."

She called up a photo of the family, looking at their smiling faces, their platinum hair, so innocent of the fate that awaited them in the icy lake.

"They do look similar to the victims. The ones that I've seen anyway, so far. Is this man trying to kill this family all over again?"

"Who wrote the article? It could be that there were some other details," Connor said. "Perhaps there was another family member involved, perhaps a jealous boyfriend, a husband who suffered guilt because he wasn't in the car? That has clear parallels to what we're seeing here. Now we need to take it further and look for the links."

Those were all good suggestions. Cami read the article again, looking for details that might be relevant. But the article was very basic. It said that they had been on their way home from a shopping trip, and that their community was left devastated. There were several quotes from people who were bemoaning that the bridge was too dangerous and that this should never have happened. That was it.

Finding nothing that raised red flags, she looked up the writer. They'd need to contact him next. Hopefully, he'd have a lot of background research that hadn't made it into this brief article, but which could provide them with a starting point.

"James McCallum, here's his name," she said. "I'm going to call him right now."

Quickly, Cami looked up James's details. But immediately, she saw there was a problem.

"Connor, look here," she said.

"What is it? Can't you find information on him?" Connor asked.

"I can. In fact, I'm finding too much. Take a look here. It seems that this writer had problems. And after he wrote this piece, these problems became serious. There's an article written on him, dated just a few months ago."

"Journalist Sentenced to Prison for Assault," Connor read, sounding surprised. "Journalist James McCallum, who worked as a freelance writer and reporter for a number of Illinois-based publications, recently was convicted for assaulting a colleague in a bar. This follows a string of offenses including DUI, petty theft, and additional instances of assault."

Reading on, Cami added, "'It seems that the strain of my job has ended up affecting my mental health.' That's what he said, Connor. That was his reason for going off the rails the way he did."

And he sure had gone off the rails. He'd committed a number of crimes that seemed to be escalating in seriousness. Topped off with a year's prison sentence. That was significant, Cami thought.

"When did he get out of prison?" Connor asked.

"The article doesn't say," Cami said after checking it.

"Let me find out then."

Now, Connor turned to his own laptop, opening it and logging into the police database. Cami felt breathless with expectation as she waited. This could be the lead they needed. Perhaps it had been that family's death that had triggered James to change the way he had done.

Perhaps it had caused a psychotic break, and he'd altered his mindset from a normal journalist to a psychopathic killer.

"He's been released on parole recently, there's a short paragraph indicating that," Connor noted.

"Being a journalist for online news sites, he would easily have the knowledge to identify and trace location pins," Cami said. "It's not difficult. He would have been able to track the victims that way, even with basic IT knowledge."

She looked at the photo of James, the writer.

He stared back at her from the shimmering screen. A man with a clean-shaven head, a frowning brow, and a cruel-looking mouth. Imagine if this was the man they'd been chasing so doggedly on his route south.

Was she looking at the killer? Had James decided to retrace or recreate the family's fate through a series of random murders?

She was sure that it was him. The more she looked at his dark, hooded eyes, the more convinced she became. He must have wanted to create his own legacy of death. And if they were right, then they were inside the mind of a serial killer.

"He looks like he doesn't like people," Cami murmured. "It all fits together. He was traumatized by the death of that family, and he suffered a mental breakdown. Then he went on a spree and killed anyone he felt deserved it." She took a deep breath. "And that's what he's doing now."

She could only imagine the darkness in this man's mind, the compulsion that he had to recreate a scene that had been so tragic, so traumatic, that it had caused his own psyche to crumble.

"Perhaps he's heading for that bridge again. If he's cutting a path due south, he might even be going back to it." She thought that was a brilliant suggestion, but Connor's headshake told her she was moving too far ahead.

"Don't jump to conclusions based on a photo," Connor warned. "He's got a long way to go before he gets to that accident scene. It's all the way south of Chicago, near the Illinois-Indiana border."

How many more kills might he need to make before he got there, Cami wondered with a chill, wishing Connor would be more open to her theory. He seemed to be far too restrained, given the urgency of the situation they were now facing.

"But it's obvious. He's working through the trauma that he suffered," Cami said, feeling frustrated that he wasn't as wedded to the theory as she was. Couldn't he see how clear the link was? "The trauma that caused this mental breakdown. He's using the people he kills to relive the experience of that family drowning. Reliving that trauma."

Connor nodded slowly. "He's a person of interest to us now, that's for sure. We need to take a closer look at him. We need to find him as fast as we can. And we need to speak to him, face to face. If he doesn't have an alibi for the killings, then we might have found our criminal."

CHAPTER EIGHTEEN

"It looks like James McCallum went back to his original place of residence after being paroled," Connor said to Cami. She watched as he accessed the FBI database to get the latest address details for the troubled journalist.

"Where's his home?"

"I'm looking now." Connor tapped his fingers on the car's dashboard as the address loaded. They were sitting in the car, ready to go as soon as they had the information they needed. Cami was sure that he must live somewhere in the wider area. After all, he reported on local issues.

"I've got the address. We'll go there right away." Connor turned to her. "He lives west of Chicago. Seems like a normal residential suburb. And he lives alone. His divorce went through recently."

Cami guessed that the divorce had been a part of the downward slide that had seen James's life crumble around him. If he was the criminal they were hunting, she felt sorry about the circumstances and the trauma that had caused it, but it still did not justify him having become a relentless killer.

"It's about half-an-hour's drive. See if you can find anything else on him in the meantime," Connor directed Cami as he started up the car and headed to the main road.

Knowing his address and his locality made the research easier. Cami had a look, digging into the neighborhood, taking a look into the online groups she could access, seeing what mention there was of this man who had transformed from a seemingly solid citizen to a criminal.

"There are actually reports of one of his crimes on a local group," she told Connor. "They discussed it and referred to it as 'shocking' and 'unacceptable'. Most people, that is. Others seemed to think that he's just very broken and damaged, and they do refer to that article as the pivotal piece that changed him."

"So, they noticed it?" Connor asked.

"Yes. And they are divided about how they see him, but it doesn't look as if he's done anything else since coming out of jail."

It was interesting to read the historic chit-chat, Cami realized. Neighborhood groups were definitely a fount of helpful information. As well as unwanted opinions, and several clear instances of defamation that she could see within a minute. *People really needed to be more careful online,* Cami thought, shaking her head at how misguided society could be when they got in front of a keyboard and had the world, or part of it, as their audience.

"He might not have had time to do anything else since he's been out," Connor said.

"If he'd been planning these crimes in jail?"

Connor nodded. "I'm the first to say, as an FBI agent, that going to jail is not the solution for everyone." He gave Cami a sidelong glance, knowing that it had almost been a solution for her.

"Really?" she asked guardedly.

"Yes, it's punishment, and it gets criminals out of circulation so they can't be a danger to society. But sometimes, people who've had mild psychological problems and go inside can come out with them worsened. For obvious reasons. If he'd been battling with that before his prison sentence, he might have tipped over the edge afterward."

"So, he might have been angry and vengeful toward society," Cami said. It was a chilling thought, to be confronted with the fact that someone with a mental health issue might be out there in the world, with only the barest sliver of control over their actions.

"Or feel compelled to recreate the scene that had affected him psychologically," Connor suggested.

Cami thought that was a very valid point. Undoubtedly, this was a highly damaged man.

He could be dangerous. And he could have killed these women, playing out the nightmare that was now lodged in his head, while heading back on a route that took him to the accident scene.

If he feels compelled to recreate the scene, then he must be thinking about that family's death. He must be thinking about what happened to them, and why it happened. He's reliving the trauma, trying to make sense of it for himself."

"And then he's taking his anger out on society by killing people," Connor said.

Cami hoped that he was right. That they'd found their criminal.

Connor slowed the car as it approached the house. Cami took a look at the street. It was a quiet, residential area, with neat houses set back from the road with well-kept gardens. She wondered what James had thought, coming out of prison and then returning to this ordered and attractive place. It clearly hadn't done much to calm his mind if he'd embarked on a killing spree.

They stopped the car outside and climbed out. They walked up the path to the door.

Cami wondered if she'd ever stop feeling a thrill of fear and anticipation at this moment, knowing that they were about to come face to face with a criminal strongly suspected of committing murder. She'd already seen how things could go wrong. She hoped this wasn't going to be another one of those times.

But it seemed that instead of a confrontation with an angry killer, they were going to be disappointed in other ways. Because nobody was coming to the door. The doors and windows of this house were closed up tightly. And it seemed that James wasn't home.

"He's not here," Connor said, sounding frustrated. "I'm going to call Ethan and see if there's any recorded place of work listed. He might even be at a parole check-in. Ironic if he went there from a killing site," he added.

"I'll keep looking online." Cami walked back to the car with Connor. Surely there must be some hint, some clue online about where this man was. He could have briefly veered back toward normality after his killing spree. He could be reporting to the police station or job hunting or visiting friends. There was nothing to stop a criminal from returning to ordinary behavior after a crime had been committed, and in fact, as she'd learned, many of them did.

So, assuming that he'd fled the latest murder scene and returned home again, where might he be now, and could she find any clue to it online?

Cami searched, sitting quietly in the car, using her laptop as well as her phone so that she had all available devices focused on the job.

She wasn't picking up anything from his own social media. That had stayed dark and unused since he'd come out of prison. People were talking about him, not to him. And not very kindly, either. Like this thread of conversation that she'd just picked up now.

"Would that be our resident parolee?"

Parolee. Cami pricked up her ears, reading more carefully. Undoubtedly, they were discussing James in this conversation thread, which looked to be current.

"I guess so."

"Doing it again?"

"Doing it again, yes."

"Should we call the police?"

"He's not doing any harm to anyone. It's wasting police time."

"He might harm himself, surely?"

"And your point is?"

"Look, if he does harm himself, he'll be wasting other people's time. Paramedics are also busy people."

"True, but like I say, he's there often."

"This time looks different."

What were they talking about? Cami wondered. This seemed to be something they had discussed before. So, maybe she could backtrack in the conversations and discover more.

She searched, using key words as well as the names of the people in the neighborhood who seemed to like discussing this the most frequently.

And, to her astonishment, she was able to figure out what they were referring to.

There was even a grainy photo of a featureless person, taken on a cloudy day and from a far distance. But the description of the location tied it in. It all made sense, logically. Of course he would be here. But the fact he was meant there was a risk attached. And the clock was ticking down.

"Connor," Cami said as he got off the phone from yet another frustrated call to the office. "Look here. I think I know where he is."

"Where is he?" Connor's voice sounded urgent. Cami could hear the stress and tension in his tone. He was feeling desperate now, as was she. This killer had to be stopped.

"He's at the bridge where the accident happened. Where the family's car drove off the road," Cami said, hearing the shock in her own voice. "It seems he goes there regularly," she said. "And from the conversation, he's most definitely there now."

"We need to get there immediately." Connor's voice was filled with resolve.

CHAPTER NINETEEN

Cami keyed in the coordinates of the bridge and put them up on Connor's GPS. He was already accelerating away from the suspect's home, taking them on a southerly route that led to the bridge where James the journalist turned criminal might even now be standing.

"What if he's been thinking about suicide?" Cami asked. If this man died, they would never know if he was the killer or not. And if he was innocent then there was even more reason to rush there and help him.

"We're on our way now. We'll figure something out."

"Hurry," Cami said as Connor took a sharp turn.

She was filled with dread. If he jumped into the water and drowned, their investigation might even go cold. That was unacceptable. It was becoming personal to her now.

Cami guessed that he must have been drawn back here again and again by some compulsion, some urge she couldn't understand. But she knew one thing. While they had time, they had to try to prevent him from harming himself.

Another thought came to her, chilling her as she considered it. "What if he goes back there to gain more resolve to kill again?" she suggested. "That might be the place where he relives this crime, and it keeps triggering him to murder."

"We're going to be there in five minutes," Connor said. "In five minutes, we'll be able to ask him that question." He sounded the same way Cami felt, that five minutes was too long a time. All they could do was watch the road scroll by in tense silence.

And then, the bridge came into view.

Cami was shocked by how high the bridge was. It arched over the lake, which was a sizeable drop below. It made her stomach feel queasy to imagine how the car must have skidded, slid, and then fallen, arcing down in a rush of silence before the explosion of hitting the water.

And there he was. She saw him and drew in a breath. He was standing, staring out over the water, a dark-haired man, broad shouldered, wearing a gray shirt and faded jeans.

Strong looking. Cami noticed that immediately. Without a doubt, this journalist would have had the physical power to carry his unconscious victims to the final place where he had drowned them.

Connor pulled over about twenty yards away from James. It was as if the journalist didn't even notice his arrival. The bridge was fairly busy with cars passing in both directions. But, standing on the pedestrian walkway next to the road, it was as if he didn't notice anything except the dark, cool waters of the lake below.

"James McCallum," Connor said, striding fast toward the lone man.

The disgraced journalist didn't turn around. He just kept staring out over the water.

"McCallum," Connor said more loudly, breaking into a run.

Cami's heart was racing as she rushed behind him. She had a horrible feeling that they were too late. James was going to jump. And he was going to do it now. And as Connor reached him, he did just that.

He clambered over the rail, causing Cami's heart to accelerate wildly. He stood staring out over the gray waters.

And then he let go of the rail that he was holding with his right hand. He leaned out over the water, and Cami heard a terrified, "No!" burst from her mouth.

But at that moment, Connor reached him. He grabbed the man's arm with both of his own, even as James's feet slipped off the narrow concrete shelf beyond the rail. Now James was crying out, but Cami couldn't tell if it was in terror or regret. His feet were flailing. Connor's grasp was literally the only thing between him and the fifty-foot drop to the waters below.

Cami rushed up, feeling absolutely terrified but determined to help. Now, she could see, James regretted his decision to jump. He was grabbing with his hands, desperately trying to get a hold of the rail again as Connor's iron grip kept him from the lethal fall.

But James's jacket was slipping, he dropped lower as Cami rushed up. He let out a shout that was filled with purest terror.

"I can't hold on," he gasped.

His voice was trembling. His legs made frantic, desperate movements as if he was trying to find a foothold on the smooth concrete of the bridge. Cami had to do something! She had to try to help.

Even though it filled her with a dizzying fear, and she worried she'd be dragged right over the rail herself, she leaned over, grasping James's belt. Connor got a better hold on his arm. James writhed around, this time grasping the rail tightly, and keeping the hold on his arm, Connor helped to lift the now shaking man back over the rail.

"I've got you," Connor said, his voice tight with tension. "I've got you."

With a flailing of limbs, James landed in a heap on the paved pedestrian walkway, breathing fast. Now, suddenly, he seemed to realize that he'd gone straight from one predicament into another that was potentially more serious. He stared at Connor and now there was shock and betrayal in his gaze.

"You're police! What are you trying to do? I've done nothing illegal. I'm not going back to prison!"

"Is there a reason you're scared of that?" Connor countered.

James's eyes narrowed. "I'm not scared of anything," he said, sitting up, and wiping the sweat from his brow. He looked absolutely terrified. "Except for falling," he said in a low voice.

"Might be a good thing to be a little frightened of the police," Connor said, his voice steady and even. "Especially if you've been breaking the law."

"I haven't been. I was here because I always come here. I feel drawn to this place. To the horror of these deaths. You know about it, right? Everyone here knows about it. How the family fell. They made me do the report on it even though I didn't want to. I felt unprepared for digging into that story. And the footage—that was shocking."

"The footage? Of the accident?"

Cami glanced at Connor. There had been footage? That could be important to watch. But James was shaking his head.

"I can't show you. It was sent to me in private when I was assigned to do the story. Someone filmed it and . . . and I watched it twice, but then I deleted it off my phone."

"You did?" Cami asked.

"It was too horrible. Too traumatic."

"Can I see your phone?"

James reached into his pocket with shaking hands and took the phone out. He looked surprised to see that it was even still there, Cami thought. And so was she. It could have easily fallen out and tumbled down to the waters below.

But she still felt confident that even without the phone, she could trace the footage. This kind of footage always lurked online. It was very hard to truly erase something from the archives.

"I don't know if I want to give my phone to you," James said uneasily. Cami wondered if that was his guilt talking. Was there evidence on this phone of what he'd done and where he'd been?

"In fact, I'm not going to!" Instead of handing the phone to her, James half-turned, and in a swift, awkward motion, he flung it over the edge of the rail.

It went tumbling down. The waters below were so distant that they barely heard the splash as it disappeared from sight forever.

Cami stared in consternation at the traumatized journalist. That was destroying evidence, clear and undoubtedly. And Connor thought so too.

"You're under arrest," he said. "Failure to obey and destroying potential evidence. We're bringing you in."

As he escorted James to the car, he turned to Cami.

"I want that footage," he said. "It could be important. Find it if you can. Find it now."

CHAPTER TWENTY

The drive to the police department should take twenty minutes, Cami estimated from a glance at the GPS. But the way Connor was driving, they'd probably make it there in less than fifteen. That meant, on this twisting and turning rollercoaster ride, she had to focus on all her devices, stop them from flying into the back of the car where James was handcuffed, and work out what this video was that he hadn't wanted them to see.

Of course, there might also be other information on the phone that he didn't want them to see. She might be able to retrieve traces of that but ultimately, throwing the phone into a deep lake had put a pretty big spoke in that particular wheel.

What could she find in time before they arrived to start the questioning?

It had been a video. Most probably a graphic video, because shocking stuff that showed people dying would align with what he'd said. So shocking that it had probably been deleted from public forums if it had been played there at all. The main social media sites would have removed it. Footage that showed people plunging to their death was way too intense and disturbing. It could trigger exactly the problems their journalist was displaying now.

The news sites might have been sent it but would never have shown it.

So, it would be available underground. On people's personal devices if they'd gotten it before it was erased and saved it in such a way that it wasn't deleted when the link was.

The dark web would tell her, but she'd have to search in a specific way. Even Cami did not like going on those type of sites, the graphic sites that played accident footage where people were injured or died. It was only one step away from a snuff movie in her view.

But those sites existed. They had millions of followers.

And somewhere among them, Cami had no doubt, she would find this video.

She searched quickly. It was hard to concentrate because Connor was speeding through traffic. He was weaving through cars, making it hard for her to type. When she waited for her screen to refresh, she glanced back at James.

He was staring down, seemingly immersed in his own private world.

Cami turned back to her screens. Finally, one had refreshed. It was shortly followed by the other.

Now, the work began. Sifting through the junk, the irrelevant footage, and the torrent of information that was swirling around in the dark web, each video time consuming and traumatic to watch.

And not what she was looking for. She needed to set better parameters.

Bracing herself as Connor took yet another hairpin bend at full speed, Cami narrowed her search. To do so, she used Connor's advice. She remembered his words that once you'd been to a scene, you had important information you could use.

And so, she did. She had more details to add to the search that might be helpful.

"High bridge. Concrete ledge. Arched bridge. Deep lake. Family. Family car."

She added more and more information to the parameters that already included the place name.

And then, at last, just as she was despairing and feeling she'd have to give up, the search got results. Something flashed up. She took a look.

It wasn't what she had expected. It was blurry and faraway. There would be little detail to be made out from here. But without a doubt, it was the right location, and a car veering off of an icy road into a plunging, fatal descent.

"I've found the video," she said, just as Connor burned rubber screeching into the police department.

"Great," he said. He said it in a tone that told her he'd expected nothing less. With her brain still steaming from what it had taken, Cami felt briefly nonplussed. Connor had been so critical, so disbelieving when they'd first worked together. Now, it seemed like his expectations had veered the opposite way, and he assumed that when she got online, anything was possible.

She sincerely hoped that she never had to manage those expectations downward. She couldn't take the thought of disappointing Connor.

"We can look at it when we're done here," Connor said. "What I want to know, now, is why James threw his phone away. We need to question him on that. There's more to it, I'm sure."

He let James out of the back seat. Grasping him firmly by the arm, he escorted him into the police department. Processing and searching him was done quickly and efficiently. Cami was hoping that when his pockets were turned out, she might see one of those blue wristbands or the red earrings that might depict location pins. But there was nothing like that on his person, to her disappointment.

And then, a minute later, he was seated in an interview room, looking forlorn and hollow cheeked as he faced Connor and Cami sitting opposite.

The room was airless. The mirrored window, Cami knew, offered access to an observation room where most likely at least one cop was waiting and watching. The recorder was working.

At last, their biggest suspect was firmly in the spotlight.

Connor began. "The phone. Why did you throw it away?"

"I'm sorry about that," James mumbled.

"Trust me, we are too. But it's not an apology I want. It's an explanation."

James shook his head. "I can't tell you. I'm sorry. I just can't. The whole thing was too traumatic. I don't want to think about it. I didn't want you to find it again. I'm not on an even keel at the moment. I thought that seeing that video would throw me off kilter again. I didn't want you to find it. Assuming it was searchable on my phone even after I erased it."

"And it wasn't like you didn't want us to know what else was on there?"

James shook his head. "It's my phone. Just my phone. There's nothing on it I need."

"Really?"

"All the work stuff, such as it is, is backed up. And I realized I didn't care about anything else."

"What do you mean?" Connor's voice was like steel.

"All my photos, my old stuff is before . . . before things went wrong. As I was thinking that, I thought throwing it away would be a good thing. Like a gesture."

Connor shook his head. "I don't believe you."

"Why not?" James's voice rose anxiously.

"Because it's too fortuitous."

"What do you mean by that?"

Connor folded his arms.

"We've had a series of murders. From north in Milwaukee, heading down south toward where you live and where the accident occurred. It's clear that the victims were identified using their location pins. They advertised where they would be."

James had gone very pale.

"What's that got to do with me?"

"Isn't it obvious?"

"No! It's not obvious at all!"

"You tracked them. That's why you threw your phone away. You're obsessed with this accident scene, to the point of coming to revisit the site. All the victims of the recent murders resemble the victims of the original crash."

"But . . . but that wasn't me!"

"You just threw away the proof that could have cleared you. So, we're assuming the opposite."

Now, James's face was set in harsh lines of panic. "Look, I didn't know. I didn't know that. I acted emotionally. I'd just tried to throw myself off the bridge, for heaven's sake. I wanted . . . I wanted to show you that I'd give you a slap in the face if you tried to force me to comply."

"Why would you have thought we needed to force you?"

James was breathing roughly. Desperate, and with a different look in his eyes from what had been there at the bridge, he said, "Because I wasn't thinking clearly. I'm still not. But if you need to know where I was and when, you don't need my phone for that. I can tell you. I will tell you. You'll see that I'm innocent!" he shot defiantly at Connor.

Connor didn't look in the least impressed by his bluster.

"Let's put that to the test, then," he said calmly.

CHAPTER TWENTY ONE

Cami didn't know if she believed that James McCallum was suddenly choosing to cooperate. This was too much of a turnaround. And he was too much of an unstable character. She could see, from the deepening crease in Connor's forehead, that he thought exactly the same.

Still, she was glad that James was talking. She wanted to know what he had to say.

James took a deep breath and began, "I want to ask you to try to understand why I did what I did. The original crash, the original accident, it destroyed me. Look, I was on the edge anyway. I had problems. I'm not going to hide it from you, because I am sure you can find out if you don't know already. I'd been taking drugs. I'd been associating with people in the underworld. It was my job to do it. I had to investigate them. That's part of what being a journalist is about. But I started getting drawn into things. I became involved."

"I understand you were not a stable character," Connor agreed.

"And then, that accident. It was hideous. I didn't know the family at all, but when I tried to start doing the research, it brought so many of my monsters to the fore. I was in a dark place. I was in a very dark place."

He gripped his forehead. He was sweating. The room wasn't that warm. Either he was seriously traumatized, Cami thought, or he was guilty. She had no idea which one it was.

"You're saying that having to report on this accident changed you?" Connor said. Cami could tell that he was trying to get a grip on exactly what this incident had meant for the troubled journo.

"It was the trigger. I was having problems before that, but they were worse after. I couldn't sleep. I couldn't eat. I couldn't work. I tried. I really did. I tried to get my job done. I tried to report, but I couldn't. It was like that accident tripped a switch in my mind. I was too busy thinking about it, obsessing about it, to focus. I know, it was unhealthy. But I couldn't help it. I was ill. Mentally. And I'm still not well."

"So, are you saying that from the time you were asked to report on this accident, you were no longer fully mentally functional?"

"Yes."

"What about your memory? Any gaps?"

Cami liked how Connor had led around to that.

"Of course there were gaps. I was on all sorts of substances I regret now. There were plenty of gaps. I couldn't cope. I couldn't handle it. I was seeing the accident replayed in my mind. I was seeing the family going off the bridge. I was seeing them die."

His voice broke. He rubbed his face with his hands. "I . . . I wasn't the same after that. I kept having nightmares. I couldn't get it out of my mind. I thought I was going crazy. I had fights with people. Took things too far. I took drugs to try to forget. I tried to keep going, to hold onto my job. But it was impossible."

James's body slumped. He had covered his face with his hands. He was rocking back and forth. Cami had a sense that he was genuinely trying to convey the depth of his distress. She really wanted to believe there was something to that.

Connor, on the other hand, wasn't going for it. "So, did your memory improve in jail? Or did you still have memory gaps after you were released?" he asked firmly.

Cami saw where this was going. Connor was not going to allow James's flawed recollections to substitute for actual physical evidence from his phone. Especially if he had in fact followed those location pins. Perhaps he'd identified people on social media who resembled the victims and who were easy to find and then he'd used his mapping app to trace them. There might be a record of that. If that was the case, then no wonder he'd thrown his phone away.

Connor was serious about this. He would not be swayed by sentiment and a guy who kept trying to avoid the issue. Cami was impressed.

"I had difficulty remembering because I was confused. On days when I was confused, it was worse. On days when I was calm, it would be better," James tried to explain. Now, perspiration was actually rolling down his cheeks. He wiped it away, staring at his wet fingers with a strangely blank look.

"So, I have to ask, where were you on the days and times when the murders were committed?"

"What . . . what are those days and times?"

"Let's start with late last night. Say, sometime from late afternoon to midnight. Can you account for your time then?"

"That's a big stretch of time."

"Can you account for it?" Connor was relentless.

"No. I didn't have anything going on yesterday. I drove around for a while. I was confused yesterday. Yesterday was not a good day. I was feeling very stressed. Regretful."

"So, you can't account for your time all day?"

"No. I can't. And I wasn't high. I've been clean since prison. I'm not stupid. But I . . . I guess I can't say where I was."

Connor's frown intensified. "You can't say where you were. Okay. Let me ask this, then. What were you doing in the days leading up to the first murder? Say, three days ago? Four days before? Is there any time in the past week or so that you truly had good recall?"

James's expression faltered. "I don't think so. This has been a very bad week. I know I had a parole check-in. That was on Monday morning. My parole check-ins are Mondays, and I know I mustn't miss them."

As she listened to James's stammering account, Cami started to feel a surprising emotion.

Pity.

She knew that it was ill advised to feel sorry for a suspect who was highly unstable, who had destroyed evidence, and who had no clear recollection of any of the times the murders had happened.

But she was starting to wonder what had caused him to go so badly off the rails. Had it been some other incident, had it been the gradual pressure of circumstances? Or had it been that video? Was the sight of it, and the timing, so terrible that it had mentally broken this man?

Cami decided there was only one way to find this out. While Connor was forging ahead with the questioning—his area of expertise and one where she couldn't interrupt—she could run through the footage and see if she could work out what had affected him so badly, if anything.

Unobtrusively, she glanced down at her laptop, and allowed this grainy, wavering video to play.

Frowning down at it, Cami couldn't see anything that would have been torturously scarring, even to a damaged man. It was horrible, that was for sure. The car was driving along and then it started to slide. Cami imagined there must have been a noise, a shrill scream of brakes or tires, that had alerted the person filming, and he or she had zoomed in and focused on the car.

It had spun. It had rolled one and a half times, in an explosion of glass and twisting metal, seeming almost to go in slow motion. And then, it had plummeted off the bridge, bursting through the railing with the force of its speed, and had twisted and somersaulted down to the icy waters below.

And then the video was still for a while. Feeling as confused as James was claiming to be, Cami replayed it.

She hadn't missed anything. There was the car losing control. Spinning off the bridge. Crashing into the waters below.

But then, something else. Near the start of the video. Something that was almost invisible given the poor footage.

It was no more than a pixel.

But as Cami stared at it, she realized that pixel might make a huge difference to what had happened next. Her eyes were not playing tricks. She really was seeing what was there.

And what was there might make all the difference in the world.

She touched Connor's elbow. Mid-question, he swung around to regard her impatiently.

"I need you to see something, now. Outside," she explained.

CHAPTER TWENTY TWO

Cami got up and hurried out of the interview room with her laptop. Now that she'd interrupted Connor, she felt consumed by self-doubt. She sure hoped that what she'd seen was accurate and not just a trick of her vision or a fault in the video.

But there was something she could do about that. As she waited for Connor to wrap up inside, Cami went into a small office opposite the interview room. It contained two tables and chairs and was currently empty. Sitting at one, she looked up some online programs that could clean up grainy video. It was important that she showed Connor the clearest picture possible and that the pixel ended up being more than just a blur.

She was busy running the program when Connor barged out of the room, looking annoyed by the distraction.

"This had better be important," he said, heading straight into the office where she was.

"I'm sorry for interrupting," Cami said. "But I think it is. You have to see this."

"To see what?"

"I've just sharpened it. It's very visible now. Watch here, near the start of the video, while the car is rolling. Watch and see."

She played it again, feeling relieved that this time, the footage was sharp enough to make sense of what she'd seen.

And what she'd seen was important. Without a doubt.

The car spun, veering out of its lane. It rolled.

But as it rolled, as the car buckled and smashed, just before its final, plummeting flight off that high bridge, a small figure tumbled out. Whether it was through a broken window or the ripped windshield, Cami wasn't sure. Without a doubt, though, that figure was there.

"Are you seeing what I'm seeing?" Connor sounded incredulous.

"Yes. One of the family members was thrown out. And it looks to be the son. I'm guessing, anyway, because of what has happened now. He would have been twenty at the time, the article said. He'd be about twenty-five now. And maybe, being the sole survivor of that accident was so traumatic to him that he never got over it. Maybe it scarred him.

And that's why he's looking for his family now. But when he doesn't find them, he kills them."

Connor was silent for a long, shocked moment.

"It's clear that James McCallum couldn't have known that," he said.

"I doubt anyone knew at the time. Maybe he was concussed and had amnesia, and he left the scene, and all this was only pieced together months later," Cami said. "Maybe he was still so traumatized by this that he didn't want it publicized."

"All possibilities," Connor said. "I'm guessing that with a fall that hard, he would have been concussed. He doesn't seem to move afterward." He peered at the video again. "And yet, if he had been deceased, he would have been found at the scene. I'm guessing whoever took this video also didn't notice and rushed straight down to the lake instead of up to the bridge. That's what anyone would do if you saw a car go over."

He was silent for a long, thoughtful minute.

"I'm going to call the office and update the team. I know Ethan might not be there, because he's out on the trafficking raid. But this is vital. We need to start researching immediately. I'm going to ask them to go back over the postmortem results. Perhaps there was some evidence of a blue bracelet on one of the victims. That could give us a link."

"Can I research it too?" Cami asked.

"Absolutely," Connor said. "I'm going to go back in and interrogate James again. I want to find out if he knows this, and if he has any idea what happened to the son. But while I speak to him—yes, you can look the son up. Scour every corner of the online world," Connor directed her. "And see if you can make any sense of the pattern he's been following with these kills, knowing what we do now."

Connor got on the phone, barking out commands to whoever was in the office. And Cami got onto her laptop. She wanted to try and trace this man—starting with his name and if she could possibly do so, ending with his address and whereabouts.

They were so close to solving this case.

She just needed to keep going.

She looked back, checking the family's name. They had been the Becker family, and the son's name was Hayden. Hayden Becker. What had happened to him after the crash? Details would be sketchy because he'd clearly wanted to keep things private. He had been traumatized, injured, and must have had memory gaps that put James's to shame. But at some stage, his memory had returned, and that was when Cami wondered if he'd been triggered to kill.

But as she looked, she found that unlike his victims, the killer had remained mysteriously invisible online. She guessed that Connor's office might find address details for him. In the public domain, she couldn't find anything. It was obvious that he'd kept an exceptionally low profile after the crash. She couldn't even find a picture of him. The family's house had been foreclosed a few months after the crash. There was no mention of Hayden Becker at all.

It was as if he was invisible. As if he really had died in the accident instead of being flung to safety.

That gave her an idea.

Perhaps Hayden Becker had lived with the results of the accident for a long time, not knowing what had happened to him. And perhaps the memory gaps had started bothering him. In which case, he might have looked for help or support.

Cami's mind raced as she put together the tentative chain of logic. She didn't think that the Becker family had been wealthy. The car that had spun out over the bridge was an old, battered Honda. If Hayden had looked for help, he wouldn't have had the funds to do so easily. And since there was zero evidence of his employment, Cami was wondering if he had a job at all. Perhaps he just did part-time work. Perhaps his mental state wouldn't allow him to hold down a proper full-time job.

But even so, he might have been haunted by his demons and seeking to explore why he was the way he was. And to do that, he might have looked for help.

How did people access affordable mental healthcare if they didn't have insurance? Maybe there were records, or applications that were done. He must have done it in the state of Illinois, surely, because that's where his family had lived.

It was worth a try, anyway.

She searched through the databases that she could access. There seemed to be only a few options for affordable mental healthcare in the state. One by one, she looked through them, seeing if it was possible to access their lists. Some of them were pretty tightly locked up.

She got into one but couldn't find Hayden Becker. There was no evidence of him on the list.

She ran her programs, hoping to unlock a couple of the other lists. While the software was running, Connor strode back into the side office where she'd holed up.

"James is apparently shocked that there was a survivor of the crash. He knew nothing about it," he told Cami.

"He didn't mention it in the article," she agreed.

"He said that he never heard anyone refer to a survivor. He even asked to watch the video again."

"He did?" Cami frowned.

"Yes. He said he feels better about it this time, and that knowing someone walked away has given him renewed hope. That he's not feeling so despairing anymore, that he might be able to come back from rock bottom."

"That's good?" Cami asked tentatively.

"It's good if he's not the killer. Which I'm still not sure about. But giving him the benefit of the doubt, if he did report incorrectly on the crash, without knowing the son survived, it doesn't help us. Because there's nothing whatsoever to be found on Hayden Becker. My office has checked. No address details. No employment. No record. Nothing."

Something that Connor said gave Cami the flash of an idea.

"You know, I was wondering if he'd gotten help for his amnesia. Assuming he was concussed in the crash and suffered memory loss. And that when the memories returned, they caused psychosis, and he went looking for his family."

"That's an idea. Or rather, it would be if he existed," Connor said.

"I've been looking. I haven't found anything either. And that made me think."

Cami hesitated.

"Think what?" Connor asked.

"Think that maybe, his amnesia was so bad he didn't even remember his name. Maybe he was rushed to hospital, and he took on a different name. Maybe that's why we can't find him. Because he's been living the whole of his life, since the accident, under a different identity."

She saw the excitement in Connor's eyes as she continued. "And if that's so, we just have to fit the pieces together, and see if we can find it."

CHAPTER TWENTY THREE

Cami felt as if she'd been presented with an unsolvable puzzle. Somewhere out there was a killer, but since the accident and his serious injury, they had no way of knowing who he was, or the new identity he'd taken on. And if they didn't find out, then without a doubt, he would kill again.

After all, there had been five occupants of the car beside himself. He'd killed four people so far. If he was trying to hunt down every single person that he perceived to have been in that crash, then there was one still to go.

"He might not even stop at five," Cami said, seeing the worry she felt reflected in Connor's face. "He might just carry on, looking for people who resemble his family. He's not finding them, so he might not stop."

"Let's go over what we know about him," Connor said firmly.

"He's blond. That we know."

"We know his age. Twenty-five. And that he's tall and strong."

"He lives in this area, and he must have a car."

"And he's been able to track down all the victims."

Cami did yet another keyword search. "Amnesia." "Unidentified blond male." "Unidentified twenty-year-old." "Injured blond male." "Mystery hospital patient."

But she couldn't find anything in the news.

"If he was injured, he surely had to go to the hospital?" Connor said.

"I know, but I'm not finding anything that refers to that," Cami said. "Maybe he didn't go there. Maybe he crawled away from that crash and slowly recovered without medical attention. Or maybe someone picked him up and took him home and cared for him on their own. That might have happened, especially if he couldn't remember who he was, and he said he had no medical insurance."

Cami thought about that. It was definitely within the bounds of possibility that someone could have done such a thing. Whether they knew who he was or not.

"Maybe they read the news article that his whole family had died and didn't want to traumatize him with it," she suggested. "Maybe they thought it was best that he went forward with a new identity and new memories."

Connor nodded. "I'm finding here that things were not well with the family."

"Their house was foreclosed. Was there more that went wrong?"

"The Becker family was in dire financial straits. Now, my office has sent me through some information. It seems like the mother and the sister both had big outstanding medical bills from an earlier car crash. The father's business looks to have a ton of bad debt against it. It's on three different blacklists. He died of a heart attack a few months before this crash, it seemed, and left his affairs in a mess."

"Okay," Cami said. "So actually, if anyone realized who he was, there were very good reasons why they wouldn't have told him. Because he could even have ended up being liable for the family's bad debt."

"Yes, that's a possibility."

"Maybe his memory worked well enough for him to seek out distant family and friends, someone who knew him before the crash? And they kept it quiet intentionally, to protect him? "

Cami felt as if they were stabbing in the dark here. She knew there had to be a way of finding this out. There had to.

But there were too many possible scenarios.

She looked away from her screens, briefly glancing at Connor, who was glowering down at his own laptop, scanning the databases, as if through sheer force of will, it would be possible to find the answers.

Then, summoning all her resolve, she took another look at the community groups. Would he have joined any of them? He clearly was on social media because he had been able to identify and track the victims' locations. But that wasn't exactly helpful. He was one of millions, and she had no idea what parameters to use. They knew nothing about him.

His name wasn't Hayden Becker. He was an unidentified blond male. A mystery.

And the only way they could find him was if they learned his new name.

The police department was starting to feel claustrophobic. There was a flicker in the overhead light that she'd only now become aware of. Now, of course, she couldn't tune it out, and it was annoying her.

It was annoying her because she wasn't focusing one hundred percent on her search, Cami knew. And the reason she wasn't doing that was that she literally felt she was out of options.

"I'm looking up distant relatives. I'm not finding any locally, though," Connor said. "Why aren't you able to pick anything up online?" Now there was a note of frustration in his tone as he glanced at her.

"Because I don't know what parameters to search for," Cami shot back, annoyed by the perceived criticism.

"You don't know?" Connor said, his voice incredulous.

Cami could feel an angry flush rising up her cheeks, even as she tried to remain calm.

"I've tried them all," she shot back defensively.

"You can't have tried them all. Think, Cami. There must be something you're missing."

You? Where was the "we" in all of this? she thought irritably.

"I just need time to think. I'm doing my best."

"We don't have time," Connor said, his voice firm.

"I can't work miracles! I can find hidden information, yes. But I'm all out of miracles."

"Doing your job is not working miracles," Connor insisted.

Cami stared at him, seething.

Now they were fighting. This entire situation was devolving into a ragged search for loose ends and minor clues that didn't seem to exist, and they were sniping at each other as if this was their first day on the job together and they hated one another.

She took a deep breath. Tipped her chair back and stared in the other direction from that annoying light and those useless screens. Stared out of the window, at the trees and road beyond, trying to clear her mind.

Surprisingly, Cami found herself thinking of her probation officer, the dark-haired, rich-voiced FBI agent Jacenta.

She hadn't realized that when you committed a crime against the FBI and then struck a deal with them where you were let off, you were assigned someone as your probation officer. Jacenta had touched base in both her previous cases, and she was sure that Jacenta would be in touch again soon.

She had initially thought that Jacenta disapproved of her. She'd gotten that impression. But she hoped that she'd done something to earn the rather scary agent's respect. And now, she found herself wondering what advice Jacenta would offer her.

Firstly, she knew, Jacenta would tell her to stop fighting with Connor. That was a certainty. Jacenta would give her a lesson on anger management and conflict resolution. Cami could imagine the words she would use. It wasn't difficult because Jacenta had told her something similar in the past.

“You handle this like an adult, Cami Lark,” Jacenta would say. “There's a time and a place for letting personal issues escalate, and that is not in the middle of a murder investigation. If you're intelligent enough to be an IT expert, you're capable of defusing an argument.”

And then Jacenta might tell her to review the evidence more carefully. That was what she would probably say, Cami thought. She was a detail-oriented person.

“Go over it again, Cami Lark,” she might say. “Nobody's asking you for a miracle. But your job doesn't involve looking at things just once.”

Maybe there was a detail she'd missed.

Maybe, seeing as she was channeling Jacenta's calm wisdom, she should go back and relook at everything they had already.

"I'm looking back at the location pins," Cami said, trying a different angle. She made sure to speak in a normal voice and not in a way that would escalate the fight. "I want to double check that we haven't overlooked something."

“Good,” Connor said.

She went back, checking over the information again. She started with looking at those location pins for each victim.

Undoubtedly, Patti's information had been set to public. So had Leanne's. But what about Sally-Anne Brewster's? That was the one that intrigued Cami, because at the time, she'd wondered why this woman would set everything to public when there was no reason for it.

She checked back carefully. Thoroughly. Second-guessing herself along the way.

Now, she was looking with a different idea in mind. And that idea was that this man, Hayden Becker, was not an IT expert. Nothing pointed to it. All he was doing was following location pins. He was a troubled man with a difficult past. There was no evidence to show that he was a hacker.

So, if he wasn't a hacker, he would have had to trace the women's locations through conventional and obvious means.

And there she saw it. The mistake she'd made. The small detail that she hadn't taken into account.

"Connor, look here," Cami said excitedly. "When I was checking up on Sally-Anne Brewster, I didn't look properly at the parameters, because there was a way for me to override them. But her location pin here was set to friends and contacts. It wasn't public."

"What does that mean?" Connor asked, a note of hope in his voice to replace the earlier antagonism.

"It means that whoever traced her must have been a friend or a contact. There's no other way they could have seen her whereabouts from outside that circle, without some serious hacking skills. So, he's far more likely to have been a friend or a contact of Sally-Anne, especially if he does live nearby here."

"So, if we look through her friends and contacts?"

"We should find him there," Cami said.

CHAPTER TWENTY FOUR

It was their only hope. This was the break in the case, the detail that Cami was pinning everything on now. Sally-Anne's recent locations had been set to friends and contacts only. So, for the killer to have seen them, he had to be connected to her.

And out of all of them, Sally-Anne had the smallest group of contacts. She wasn't famous, or high profile, or a relentless self-promoter, like Leanne and Patti had been.

Now, they needed to see who her friends and contacts were. And for this, Cami had a very useful piece of code that she'd gotten a while ago off open source and had stashed away, thinking it would be something that might come in handy one day. It was called Connection Crawler.

It automated the process of finding lists of mutual friends and contacts. It changed it from a tedious, time-consuming process, to one that took a couple of minutes. This software would scan the friends in common and compile a full list of Sally-Anne's connections, even though Cami was not direct friends with Sally-Anne herself.

"I've got a program here that's going to be able to search all her friends and connections. I'll send you a list as soon as I have it."

"How many people will it be?"

"It looks like only a few hundred. So within those, we need to search for the one we want. The age, the looks, the hair color. That should narrow it down."

Cami took a look at the list as the program obediently worked, the names flipping down, one after the other. Each one was a prospect that could help them solve this case. Carefully, she searched through, looking for the right parameters. Looking for the killer.

There were only a few men of the right age who were Sally-Anne's friends.

Then the name leaped out at her.

"Becker Evans," she said aloud.

"What? So, he used his family's last name as his first name?" Connor asked.

"Maybe he remembered it, or he wanted the connection, even if it wasn't obvious. But it's him, I think. Becker Evans is the right age, and he lives locally. I'm going to see what he looks like now and compare him to the old photos of the family."

Cami searched online, looking for a photo.

"He doesn't have many photos of himself online at all. But there is one shot that matches up. The features look the same, except now, he has a scar on his head." She could see the red, raised mark clearly on one of his blond temples. "I think he had a severe injury, and it might have affected him from then on," she said.

"Let's get his address," Connor said. "Car number plate details. I'm connecting with the office. They can research those things. But that's not all we need." He stared at Cami. "An address might not be helpful to us at this time. We need to know where he's headed. Because this man is clearly not staying home. He's on a mission. He's literally moving from kill to kill with barely a break. And by now, it's likely he's going to be on the move again."

Cami nodded. Worry twisted inside her. It wasn't enough to find Becker Evans. They had to find the last link, the final piece to this puzzle, the killer's next target. And she knew that if they didn't hurry, then based on the frequency of his kills so far, he would take another victim.

"I have two ideas," Cami said. "Because I see here that Becker connected with all his victims. He was friends, or a follower, or a liker of all of them. He does have a connection with every person he's killed so far."

"So, what can you conclude?" Connor asked.

"My programs can use this information. I'm going to run two different ones. The first is an algorithm that I'm setting up. I'm going to see if it can pick up any patterns to his movements that we haven't seen so far, and then I'll feed that back to us. If it works, we might be able to predict where he's going to go next."

"That algorithm sounds good." Connor nodded. "As soon as I have his address details, you can feed it in."

"Yes. That'll be important. It'll help it work better for sure knowing where he's based."

"And the second? You said you had two ideas?"

"The second is to look through Becker's friends and connections. Because he will be targeting his next victim from them. So, we need to look for someone who fits the right profile and who's in the area where he will be going next, according to his pattern."

Cami ran her crawler program again. She was now looking to unearth the private list of Becker's connections. Those he knew and that he'd connected with. Because within them, his next target could be waiting.

"Okay," Connor said, sounding motivated. "I've got an address for him. He lives at 40 Spruce Gardens, in an outlying suburb of Chicago."

"I'm looking it up now. It's a low-cost apartment block," Cami said.

"I think that aligns with what we concluded about the accident," Connor said. He's not a high earner. He doesn't seem to have significant IT expertise. He's just looking to trace people who resemble his dead family, by fairly basic means."

Now that they were making progress, the friction between them had gone. Cami felt like they had a chance now. She added the address to the algorithm and let it do its work, watching the program run, hoping that the results it would bring them would take this forward.

Connor got on the phone again to his team in the office and Cami felt grateful that they were doing some of the legwork. This time, he was finding out the registration details for Becker's car. But that didn't seem to be as easy.

"I'm not picking up anything for a vehicle," he said, sounding as if he was about to lapse back into irritability. "It could be that he's rented or borrowed a car for this mission, or even stolen one. Who knows? But there isn't a vehicle registered in his name."

That was a big setback, Cami knew. A car registration and a vehicle description would have been very helpful. Connor wasn't giving up, though.

"I'm going to see if my office made any progress with getting the two sets of camera footage from the two different scenes. If they have that by now, or it's coming soon, that could help us. So, how's your program doing?"

He pressed his lips together, glancing again at Cami's laptop.

"It's running. It's running, I promise. As fast as it can," she assured him.

She was also staring at the laptop as if her own gaze might help the programs go faster, but she knew that they were working at maximum speed already. They couldn't go any quicker than they were. They were good programs. This was top drawer coding. She'd gotten it and tweaked it, and she knew that it was going to be as effective as it could.

When it finally threw out a result, of course. Until then, they'd just have to sit and wait. That applied to her. Connor was now standing up and pacing.

"Your programs. Can they run in the car?"

"Sure. They can. I just need to keep the devices open," Cami said.

"Let's head out. I feel that we're wasting time here. We can at least go in the direction of his house. Perhaps there's a clue there, something we can use. Perhaps there's that tiny chance he might still be home. I'll ask the local cops to process James McCallum's release, but to ask him to stay in the local area with his phone open in case we need to speak to him again."

"Let's do that," Cami said. She also felt glad to be going somewhere and getting out on the road. It felt as if, that way, they were at least getting a step ahead.

After organizing James's release with the local police, they climbed into the car. Connor set off, heading for the apartment, which was in a rundown area to the south of Chicago, Cami saw.

She kept checking her devices. Surely, by now the program should have wrapped up. She felt impatient as if time was bleeding away and there would soon be none left. Where was he now? Where was he heading?

And then, abruptly, the program ended. Cami stared down and took a look at what the results were.

"Connor, we're going in the right direction," she said. "But we'll need to go further if he's targeting one of his connections."

"Why?" He braked sharply.

"I've got the map and the friends list. Based on the two programs, the comparisons between them, and the description of the victims he's choosing, my software is telling me there are two people he could be targeting next. I don't know which one of them it will be."

"Tell me about them?" Connor said, as he swung the car in a U-turn, accelerating the other way.

"One is Meryl Steele. She lives a few miles south of Becker. She's a housewife, it looks like. She's blonde, in her forties, and she pins her location. She's home now. And the other is someone he has followed for a few weeks now. She's Jayne Bell, a model coach. She's in her forties also. Very glamorous, very fashion focused. She lives about twenty miles south of Chicago, in a smaller town. She's currently in the local school, doing coaching."

"And your algorithm can't tell which one is more likely?"

"No," Cami said, feeling frustrated. "The geolocation is too inconsistent. There's no set distance or route, it's just a southerly trajectory. He seems to be basing this more on the victims he's identifying along the way, than the places."

"Right. So people are his thing. As long as the places are within the ballpark, it works for him?"

"Yes. That seems to be his priority."

"I guess it's about the people. That's what he's trying to find. So, which one do we choose?" Connor tapped his finger thoughtfully on the wheel, glancing at the two locations.

"I'm going to go with the closer one," he said. "Let's go to Meryl Steele. I'll ask the local police to go to Jayne Bell. If she's twenty miles away, then they'll be able to get there before we will."

He swung the car along a side street, speeding to the suburb where Meryl Steele lived, barking out commands into the radio.

Cami kept her programs running and tried to keep a watch on both the women. She still felt an uneasy twist of her stomach when she thought about where they were, because in the past, he'd often targeted his victims shortly after they had traveled or moved.

She didn't want to rely on these two locations alone. If the killer had done basic research on his next target, he might know something about her movements that they didn't know.

At that moment, Connor's phone rang again, and he picked up, speaking to the office.

"Yes? Any news?"

He switched the phone to speaker so that Cami could hear.

"We looked up the postmortem results for the Becker family accident," the agent back in the office said.

"And? Anything to be found?"

"As you know, there were only five people in the vehicle. Not six. That's confirmed. And the mother, who was driving, was wearing a blue armband, similar to the ones that have been found at the scenes."

"Thanks," Connor said. "That's a help to us."

The mother? Cami felt shocked.

This confirmed to her, for certain, that the killer was trying to play the accident scene out in his tortured mind again.

CHAPTER TWENTY FIVE

The lost man knew that this was the most important target yet. This was the last one he had to choose. After this, it didn't matter. He would have finished the search for his family.

His family. The words sounded strange. It was only recently that he'd remembered he even had a family. He'd forgotten they existed. He'd forgotten so much.

It had all come back to him, of course. First in snippets, and then suddenly, in a rush, he'd remembered all of it.

Before the memories had returned, all he'd known was the face of the bearded man who'd found him in the woods.

"Who? Who are you?" There had been a gun pointed at him. He'd known what it was of course, but even that word had taken a while to filter through to his mind.

All he could do was stammer out a name that came to him, from somewhere, but he didn't know where.

"Becker. Becker."

"Becker? You a runaway? Been in a crash? A fight?"

His head was hurting. The man was frowning, his tanned forehead creased, looking at a point on his temple, with some concern.

"I don't know."

"You got family?"

"I don't know."

The man's eyes widened with some surprise. "You don't know? You don't know who your family is?"

"No."

"You got no ID? No wallet? No cell phone?"

"No."

"You remember anything at all?"

"No. No, I don't."

"You sure? You in trouble? I think you are."

"I don't remember."

The man had waited a minute and then sighed. His voice had been sympathetic.

"You've had a bad time of it. You need to come with me, I'll get you some help."

The man reached to try and help him up. He'd staggered to his feet. He'd felt dizzy and weak and bruised in a hundred different places.

"We don't trust the police in our group. We're a private militia. But we can get that cut on your head cleaned up and then, if you work, you can pay your way for a while. We have lots of jobs to do. Building, construction, tree felling. We can always use extra hands."

The man who had found him had been kind, at first. The militia unit had given him a chance, a place to stay.

He was doing a job, the man had told him. He was helping the country. He had to be careful, he had to be vigilant, he needed to watch for what was wrong and what was dangerous.

And it had seemed true. He'd lost everything else. He couldn't remember anything. His name. His family. His home. No one knew who he was, and some people thought he was dangerous.

"We'll make you useful again," the man had said. "We'll teach you some skills, so you can support yourself with hard work. You'll be free to leave after you've paid us through that work."

He'd gone along, and that had become his new life for a few years. The group, which comprised about fifty men and a few women and families, prioritized discipline. Every moment, every action, and seemingly every thought he'd had were policed. Even though from time to time, in his dreams, there were memories.

Memories of a family he had never known. Sisters. Memories of something else. A terrible accident. A car overturning. The crack of something hard, hitting his head.

But he'd never had a chance to worry about those nightmares, because he'd been kept busy and controlled. He'd spent his days working in the grounds, cutting grass, and maintaining machinery. In return, he'd received food and clothing and training in manual skills. He became a competent bricklayer, he could do basic plumbing, and he was able to grow vegetables and tend the soil. He had been quiet and obedient, even though from time to time, strange and devilishly violent thoughts had flitted through his mind. Under the strict supervision of his bosses, though, he knew better than to act them out.

When there had been a change in leadership, the new militia head had given him a choice. Join us as a full member, or else, you can leave on good terms.

Uncertain, but curious to revisit the world outside of those walls, he'd chosen to leave.

But outside of the walls had been more difficult to cope with than he'd expected. Spending his days in idleness, without the routine and activity, had left him feeling adrift. He'd gotten a few jobs, lost a few jobs, but he'd realized that his personality was slowly changing into someone different. Perhaps, the same someone he'd always been.

First slowly and then faster, the memories had seeped back. For some reason, being alone had accelerated their return.

And the memory that he couldn't bear to think of, the one that troubled him the most, was the worst one of all.

He'd been in trouble on that car ride. He'd been caught stealing something. It hadn't even been to help the family. It had just been petty theft. He'd taken a pair of sunglasses from a display outside a store in a shopping mall. But the family was in trouble. They were suffering, in hardship. The home was being foreclosed, and the appliance repair business was failing. It had been in trouble even before his dad had died. And now he had stolen, which his mother seemed to think was the worst crime of all.

And yet, to him at that moment, it seemed as if it was all his fault. He was the one getting shouted at. He was the one getting victimized. He'd gotten angry, and the rage had felt like a torrent that was swallowing him up.

He remembered the moment when it felt as if something within his brain had snapped. That was the time he had suddenly realized he couldn't take it anymore.

Becker had felt a vicious need for revenge, to stop his mother's diatribe, even if it ended up destroying him as well.

He had leaned forward from the back seat where he'd been pinned between his aunt and his sister, with his mother screaming at him from the driving seat and his big sister turning around to look at him in worry and distress.

He had grabbed the wheel, pulling it away from her. He'd seen her try to grasp it. He'd seen her wrist in such detail, the blue wristband around it, the red flash of her beaded earring. And he had twisted it as hard as he could. He hadn't been thinking beyond that, not any further, but he'd known with vicious triumph this would be enough to shut the old lady up at last.

Screams had filled the car as it had started to skid, hitting ice, whirling off the road, the trajectory sudden and violent and uncontrollable. It had tipped and rolled. A chaos of crashes, smashes, and screams.

And then, nothing. Only the blacktop, hitting his head, annihilating the memories. Nothing. He had no idea how he'd moved from the road, and he guessed that would always be a blur.

He'd killed his whole family by twisting the wheel. That, he now realized. That was what he'd pieced together.

But if he could only find them, if he could get to people who were close enough, he felt certain that he could bring them to life again. He needed to do it because the pain inside him was almost unbearable. He had to find a way to make it all disappear.

In the end, it only took a few days to find his first target.

It had been a few days of remembering, and a few days of piecing together the details, the social media sites, the friends, and the locations. They were all there. He wasn’t much of a planner; he was more of a spur of the moment kind of guy. But he'd learned to be patient. He'd learned to prepare. He had learned some very useful skills in the militia, even though he couldn't say he'd made any friends. That was a skill he didn't seem to know about.

He'd learned to become stronger than anyone could imagine.

Now, the man checked his phone and climbed into his borrowed car, smiling as he confirmed where he was heading. He had no doubt that his next target would be there because he had been very careful to confirm it correctly. That was one thing he found he was good at.

It was only after he'd left the militia that he had realized there were other social connections to be made, outside of friendships and groups. Online connections. He could follow people without them knowing it. That was fascinating to the lost man. Fascinating and strangely compelling. As his network slowly expanded, he realized that there were people out there who resembled his family.

Perhaps that was also what had triggered his memories. The first time he'd seen someone on social media who resembled his dead aunt, it was as if part of that memory had been unlocked. And from there, it had snowballed. And within the rush of memories, his plan had come to him. It was a brilliant plan. He felt totally confident it would work, but it relied on him following it through.

At first, the kills had felt strange. Later, though, he had found them satisfying.

He was looking forward to reaching this last destination. He checked the location pin. As he thought. His final victim was on the move.

And when she got to where she was heading, he would be waiting.

CHAPTER TWENTY SIX

While she and Connor were speeding toward Meryl Steele, Cami couldn't shake the feeling that they were missing an important detail. That there was going to be something this killer knew, and they did not.

Yet again, she checked her programs. They had identified only two potential victims, but it was always possible that he had changed his parameters slightly and was following a third.

Cami told herself that she had to trust his patterns, and she had to trust her program. There was nobody else she'd been able to identify who fitted the right description.

Connor's phone rang. Steering with one hand, he grabbed it. "Yes?" Quickly, he thumbed it onto speaker so that he could turn more accurately through a twisting series of bends.

"Connor? Can you talk?" The voice was unknown, and Cami's mind flitted immediately to Ethan. She hoped that he was okay. The few cases she'd been on had made her realize what a high level of risk was involved in every single criminal chase down. Busting a trafficking ring sounded dangerous.

"Hi, Ben. I'm on the road," Connor said. "About five minutes away from the possible victim's residence. You got anything?"

Cami realized that Ben must be one of the team assessing the footage back in the FBI office.

"We're trying to narrow it down," Ben explained. "We have the two sets of footage. They've just come in, but a section of one of them is corrupted, so we have to request it again."

"You know the approximate times," Connor said. "The aquarium will give you the narrower time frame, so look there first."

"We'll do just that, boss. I've identified the times, and we're searching within those parameters right now. As soon as we have the updated footage, we'll hopefully be able to see if there's a match."

"Excellent. Call me if you get results. I'll call you if anything changes."

Connor hung up and turned to Cami. "We've got somewhere to start with the vehicles. That might narrow down the search."

Cami tried to push down the feeling of unease that was creeping inside her. She knew that she had to think ahead and had to focus on what was waiting at Meryl Steele's place. The local police would hopefully be at Jayne's house within the next few minutes. With any luck, both these women would be safe. And now, at least they knew who their killer was. With his identity and his home address now confirmed, it would be far easier to track him down.

But she couldn't suppress the bubbling fear that they were going to be too late to prevent yet another death. That this man, with his damaged mind, his violent tendencies, and his basic knowledge of IT and social media, was still going to be ahead of them. That even with all her knowledge and skill and Connor's speed and expertise, they were going to be too late.

"I'm feeling really nervous," she shared to Connor as they drove. He glanced at her, and she continued, "I don't know why. I have a very bad feeling about this."

"Why? You think you've missed something?"

"Yes. I'm worried he knows something we don't. I've run my programs over and over. There are only these two women. My parameters can't pick up anything else, and yet, I don't know if we are going to be in time. Is that crazy?"

"You might just be nervous. You've done a few cases now. When you start out as a rookie, you have no idea what's happening. It's only with experience, when you start realizing the complexities and what can go wrong, that you get scared," Connor admitted.

"I hope so." But privately, Cami worried that her instinct was telling her something for a reason.

"We're close. We should get there in time."

"I know. I just keep thinking of the last time when we were too late. I can't get rid of the worry that we're going to be too late again."

"We'll get there in time," Connor repeated. "We have to."

"I hope you're right. I'm just nervous. I don't know why."

"You'll be fine. You've got this."

Cami nodded. She tried to channel some of that confidence, but she couldn't quite manage it. She couldn't shake the feeling that her fear wasn't irrational.

"Here we are. This is her road," Connor said. "And there's her house. On the corner."

There were no other cars nearby, Cami saw. Nobody was there. The door was closed. Her stomach twisted because she knew that didn't mean they—or Meryl—were safe. It might just mean he'd already done the deed and left.

Connor parked outside, and they raced up to the door. He hammered on it.

There was a pause. A terrible, seemingly endless silence that seemed to sear Cami's soul.

Connor didn't look traumatized. He looked deliberately calm. He raised his hand to knock again.

And at that moment, the door flew open.

Cami let out a deep breath as she saw an angry-looking blonde woman standing in the doorway. She was wearing an apron and rubber gloves. Cami had the impression that she'd been interrupted in a big cleaning project.

Her annoyance turned to surprise as Connor showed his badge.

"FBI. Ma'am, we're on the trail of a suspected criminal and there's a chance, based on our research, that you might be a target."

"Me?" She looked astonished. Then the light dawned. "Is this to do with these strange murders that have been taking place? I heard about them."

"Yes, ma'am. It is."

"And why should I be a target?" She frowned.

"The killer is choosing victims based on certain parameters of appearance, habits, and location," Connor explained calmly. "We've run programs to try and predict where he might be striking next, and your name was shortlisted by the program."

"How bizarre." Now, she looked worried. "Well, I guess if the program thinks he might target me, that's serious."

"Do you know a man called Becker Evans? We're seeking him for questioning."

"Becker Evans, Becker Evans." Meryl shook her head. "The name's familiar, but I can't place him. I know my nephew has many friends in this area, and quite often when I get friend or connection requests, it's through him. I do gift packs for a lot of local stores and events, you see."

Cami guessed that if Becker had targeted this woman, he'd taken care to stay under Meryl's radar. It seemed that he didn't get to know his victims before he tracked them, but only targeted them based on the kills he was planning.

"Ma'am, I'm going to ask a favor," Connor said. "Until we have closed this case, there's a chance you might be at risk. I'm going to ask the local police to come here and wait inside your house to provide you with protection."

"Inside the house?" Meryl looked surprised.

"It's important that they stay as close as possible and provide a visible deterrent to the killer as well as active, on-site protection to you."

"So, you mean I've got to clean with a policeman watching?" She looked perturbed.

"Until we have more information on the killer's movements, yes."

"Oh, I'm sure I can manage without that. I mean, my neighbors and I look out for each other, and I'll keep the door locked." She clearly didn't like the thought of a cop on-site, interrupting her privacy and cleaning work.

"Ma'am, it's important that we keep you safe. A neighbor might not be in time to stop this from happening. These crimes have occurred very fast. This is our job, and we're trained to do it. I promise that the policeman will leave as soon as we have an update on where the criminal is."

Meryl sighed. "All right, then. Better safe than sorry, I guess."

"Exactly, ma'am. I'm going to call the local police to come around here immediately. Thank you for your cooperation."

As Connor turned away, Cami could see that the woman was mentally preparing herself, mentally accepting the need for protection. She guessed that it took a leap of logic to accept that you were in danger. It was easier just to deny it and to believe everything would be alright.

But right now, if the killer arrived, Meryl would be protected. Connor was already on the radio, calling for reinforcements.

And his phone was ringing. That made her nervous. Were they calling to say they'd caught this killer at the school where Jayne was teaching modeling?

He answered, frowning.

"Cami," he called. "Come quickly. There's been a development. And this could be serious."

CHAPTER TWENTY SEVEN

"Jayne Bell has left the school grounds," Connor told Cami, and she felt cold inside at the words. "The local police called the school immediately, but there was a delay as there was no phone connection to the outside hall where she was teaching the modeling course. By the time the message had been communicated and the school had sent someone to go and look for her, the class had finished, and she'd gone."

"Where? Where has she gone?" They were both rushing to the car. Cami couldn't believe this. It was exactly what she'd been dreading. That the killer knew, better than they did, where she was headed.

"Apparently, she goes for a hike in the woods after she's finished her lessons. She walks to the school as it's close by where she lives."

They scrambled into the car. Connor headed off. This distance—now closer to ten miles than twenty from Meryl's house—still felt impossibly long.

"Can they phone her?"

"They're trying. She's not picking up. They think her phone's on silent after the lessons, and she hasn't switched the ringtone back on."

"Can we track the phone?" Now Cami was feeling as if this was her worst nightmare come true.

"My office is on it. They're setting it up."

"We need to get there," Cami said.

"I know. We're not far away. I'm getting a visual description of what she's wearing any moment." The radio crackled. "Wearing black leggings and a gray top." He sighed. Cami guessed he'd wished for pink, or something that would be more visible from a distance in the woods.

They drove for the next few minutes in silence. Connor's face looked set and stern. He was clearly equally worried about this new development.

"Where does she go after the hike? Straight home?"

"Yes. The school thinks so, anyway."

"He could be waiting there."

"Not anymore. Police are at her home already." The radio crackled as Connor accelerated onto the highway. "No sign of her. No sign of him."

"He's tracking her in the woods. I know he is. He must have watched her routine before now and known which way she goes." Cami felt panic fill her. This was what he was going to do. He'd taken Leanne while she was out hiking on the trails. The same would happen here to Jayne.

"We're almost there," Connor said as he pressed down on the gas pedal.

Cami was biting her lip. She couldn't stop thinking about the horror of this scenario and what it would bring. Jayne was an innocent woman who did not deserve to die at the hands of a psychopath. Surely, they could save one, just one, from this lethal killer.

"What's the plan?" she said.

"If we haven't been able to track her, then we search. We have three police who've just arrived on site at the closest trail head and are waiting for us. That's where we're going to set this up."

Cami had her phone open but didn't know what she could do with it—if anything. There might be nothing she could do. She checked Jane's social media again, read closely through today's updates. And yesterday's. She hadn't mentioned a walk in the woods. Surely, there had to be a way of finding where she was. She needed to think, think as fast as she could, because they had arrived.

There, ahead, she saw the gate to the school, winding up through the treed hills. And on the other side, the entrance to the forest trails. A police car was waiting there.

Connor jumped out of the car and strode over to the cops. They already had a map of the trails unfolded on the hood of their car. Scrambling out of the passenger seat, Cami hurried after them.

"There seem to be two main routes here. The northern one and the eastern one," the cop explained. "Both lead to a main path that passes her house. Both pass several rivers, and the routes run each side of a small lake."

Cami knew that meant there would be water available and close by for him to drown his victim. This would happen fast. There wouldn't be time, and they might already be out of whatever time they were going to get. She felt as if they were living a nightmare. It felt like they were trying to stop a runaway train that was already speeding lethally out of control.

"Right. Let's split up. We're going to take one of the main pathways each. We need to be on the lookout for a hiker fitting his description. Any parked cars should be treated with suspicion and checked out. He must have parked somewhere nearby." Connor glanced at his phone again. Cami guessed that he was looking for any messages, any updates that might give a clue about the killer's car.

"Nothing from the camera feed yet," he said. "But they're working on it now. They might get a result in a few minutes, or it could take another hour."

So, it looked like they weren't going to get lucky there. Finding the killer's car via the camera feeds might not be possible in the time available, and Cami guessed that they'd just have to resign themselves to that fact.

"Shall we start out?" the other cop said.

Cami was sure that she would be deployed in Connor's group, but she was wrong. He turned to her, his face serious. "I want you to stay here," he said. "Lock yourself in the car. Two in each group is enough. If you can do any research on site using your devices, make any progress with where she might be, I need you to do it and to tell us."

Cami tried not to feel disappointed. Holing up in the car, doing her research, tracking the killer through her IT expertise, was her strength. Walking out on the trails in pursuit of the killer was most definitely not her strength, and she knew that in these situations, a pair of cops was generally the most effective.

But in this critical situation, she wanted to be out there. She wanted to tread impatiently along the trail, each step potentially taking her closer to the killer. It felt futile to lock herself in the car. Cami wanted to argue it, but she knew that would be pointless too. Because someone had to keep checking for clues online, even if there didn't seem to be any. And that someone was her.

Connor strode off into the forest on a trail that led north, walking shoulder to shoulder with his new partner. The other cops set off to the east, and Cami watched them both go. Her stomach flip-flopped with tension. She tried to tell herself that there was no reason to worry. Even if the killer was here, Connor was good at his job. He would be able to handle it.

But what if the killer had come and gone already?

Of course, there was always the more reassuring option that he had never intended to target Jayne at all. He might have been trying to track Meryl and that seeing the cops outside her door had put a spoke in the wheel. He might be ducking and diving in a panic now, knowing they were on his trail.

But he might also be waiting in the woods, ready to kill again, and Cami feared that was the more likely option.

She got back into the car, locked the door and sat back. She would do what she could.

Inside the car, she opened her laptop and began to work through all the information she had on Jayne Bell. She scrolled through the woman's social media again, scouring the pages, looking for anything that might help her pinpoint where she would be.

As she did that, her phone rang. It was Ethan. Her heart quickening, she picked up. She'd been worried about Ethan. It was good to see him calling.

"Hey," she said. "Are you okay?"

"Hey, Cami. We just finished the takedown. Got both of the bad guys in custody. No injuries to any agents. So, it went well, and I'm on the way back. Just checking in to see how you're doing?"

"I'm frustrated. We've worked out who the next victim probably is. But she's out walking somewhere in a network of trails. Her phone's on silent and they haven't been able to track her geolocation yet."

"There's a problem with that system. It's down in a lot of places at the moment, and it also caused us to have snarl-ups and delays. But that's a huge problem for you now. So, she's out there somewhere, and you don't know where?"

"Connor and three other cops have gone out searching. They've left me here to trace him online, but I don't know where to look or how he's planning his next kill, if he is at all. I need to think!"

Ethan sighed. "That's big pressure, Cami. How's he doing it? The last I heard, he was using location pins?"

"Yes, he is. But this woman, Jayne, is out for a walk and nobody seems to know where. The problem is that I'm sure he knows."

"How can he be doing it then? Does he know her habits? Could he have done surveillance on her before now?"

"He hasn't physically tracked any of his other victims, that I know of. He seemed to know where they would be via their location and pin drops. And he's not the greatest at IT. He's not a hacker. Just an ordinary user."

As she was doing this, a thought occurred to her.

If Becker had used information that was available online, Cami needed to use his logic and trust in it. She had to assume that he had been following clues that Jayne had left online. And that just meant she needed to look for them. They couldn't be that hard to find, surely? This killer hadn't used expert tech skills to track any of his prey so far. But what he had used was eluding them. Why?

“It must be obvious, then,” Ethan said, confirming what Cami was thinking. His voice was so calm and reassuring. She felt bolstered by his support. And, as Cami thought about it, she realized what the answer might be.

Of course, she thought. It was obvious. In fact, it was so plain and simple that they hadn't gone looking for it—yet.

"Ethan, while we were speaking, I’ve had an idea. I think I know where to look, and how he found where she would be. So, I’d better go now, and see if I’m right.”

“Good luck,” Ethan said, sounding excited.

Cami cut the call. Quickly, she began checking where she needed to, to see if her hunch was correct.

CHAPTER TWENTY EIGHT

Connor paced through the forest, checking left and right, referring frequently to his map. He kept his gaze constantly roaming. Black leggings, gray top. Blonde hair. That was what he was looking for. And, of course, for an anonymous blond male attacker, hiding somewhere in these woods.

"She has to be on one of the two trails, surely?" the cop partnering him said. He spoke the words in an urgent voice as if he was hoping that by saying them, they would be true.

"Logically, yes," Connor replied. But just as he knew Cami had done, he was feeling an uneasy sensation that there was something they were missing. Some clue the killer knew about that they didn't.

Perhaps that was inevitable on a case like this, where this man was literally on a killing rampage. Hunting a psychopath could be a mental game, Connor knew, and it was important not to feel in your own mind that you'd lost. Second-guessing yourself could sometimes lead to failure.

Just as important was not to let the killer get inside your head. He needed to have faith in his own ability to track him down, and he also needed to have faith that Cami was doing as much as she could online. They were using every available avenue to lead them to this man.

"We'll find her," he said to the cop beside him. But he didn't feel as confident as he sounded. He didn't know why, but there was something he couldn't put his finger on that was making him feel uneasy.

The cop nodded, but Connor still felt as though he was reassuring himself.

The other cops, out on the eastern trail, were calling in every so often. But the updates so far had been brief and disappointing.

"Nothing yet," another came through.

"Nothing here," Connor replied. The forest felt warm, the trees were not letting in enough of the breeze. Insects were swarming around his head, and he batted them away. He kept his eyes open and his ears too. A sound might be the only clue they would get that the killer was nearby.

They moved on. A few minutes later, they came to a junction. To their right, the trail wound up a hill and disappeared into the trees. To the left, it ran straight.

"We might need to split up here," Connor said, consulting his map again. The uphill trail was nothing more than a faint pathway, and it looked longer. It did a winding loop around the hill before rejoining the track again.

"Yes. We should each take one route. Hopefully we connect further along."

"Hopefully."

Connor took the uphill route as the other cop moved along the straight trail. His legs were burning as he climbed, but there was no time to waste. If Jayne would only answer her damned phone, he thought, if she'd only check it and see that there were now probably ten missed calls from the police. If she'd only listen to the messages that could save her life.

If she was still alive. That thought gave him a chill.

If this went badly, he knew the responsibility would be on his shoulders. There was already a huge amount of anger and blame being generated. It made it worse that a couple of the victims were high profile. Leanne's death, in particular, had caused consternation in political circles, because she'd done so much for tourism in the area. And the murder at the aquarium had been a PR disaster for sure.

He kept his gaze moving, his senses alert, and his mouth dry. But as he moved through the trees and bushes, he had no sense that he was getting any closer to her. These trails were empty.

He told himself that it was a big forest. She might be just a few hundred yards away, among the dense trees.

But the voice of worry had begun to resound in his head. *She could be dead,* the voice said. *If the killer got to her first, she could be dead.*

Connor tried to ignore the thought. It was just a feeling, he told himself. Just a feeling and not fact. But he knew that he couldn't put it out of his head. He tried not to think of all the things that could go wrong—that could be going wrong right now.

And then, his phone started ringing. Quickly, Connor grabbed the call, his hopes surging. It was his office on the line.

"Any news?" he said.

"Yes," the agent in the office said. He sounded triumphant. "We finally got a match on the car."

"What is it?" This was huge, Connor knew. This could be their first big breakthrough.

As the agent was speaking, Connor heard the beep that indicated he was receiving another incoming call. He couldn't do anything about it, though. Not now, not while waiting for vehicle details.

"There is only one car that was in both locations at the right time. It's a white Audi SUV. I'm sending plate details through now."

"Registration details?" Connor asked.

"I'm taking a look as we speak." There was a pause. "It's registered in the name of John Knight, who is a member of a local militia group. I doubt it's stolen. It's most probably loaned, but I also doubt Knight would know the reason for Becker needing this vehicle. We know the militia group well. It is somewhat anti-establishment, but we've never had that kind of trouble from them in the past. Most likely, Becker is connected to him somehow and asked for a favor."

"I've got the plate," Connor said. "The message just came through. You need to get an APB out on this immediately. I'll tell the others."

"Will do." The agent cut the call.

Connor got on the radio.

"We've got an ID for Becker's vehicle," he said. "White Audi SUV. He read out the plate details.

Almost immediately, the radio crackled. It was the other team.

"We passed a car like that five minutes ago," the cop said, sounding excited. "It was parked up near one of the trail heads. We both saw it and made a note of the plate. The vehicle was unoccupied."

"He's here!" Connor felt breathless with tension. "What are the map coordinates? We need one officer to remain near that car in case he's on his way to it. One of you, go back."

"I'm on my way," one of the others confirmed. As for the rest of us, we might need to reroute. Where are the likely trails that he would have taken from that parking site?"

This was a huge break. They were getting closer.

"We'll need to get another team out to help us search," Connor told the rest of the team. "We might need a helicopter too."

"You think visibility is good enough?" the other cop asked.

"I know visibility isn't great in the densely wooded areas, but there are a lot of open trails nearby and down at the lake, and right now, we know he's here. The more eyes we can have on this area, the better."

He opened the map again and took a look at the coordinates of where the car was parked. How did they align with Jayne's possible routes? Given Becker had parked near the trail head, how should they reroute?

Narrowing his eyes, he tried to make what he thought was the best decision.

"I'll reroute," he told the group. "It seems like he would have had to go a mile out of his way to come up this hill. I'll backtrack and go down to the valley and take that other lower trail. It intersects with the main one further along."

Feeling as if this mission was finally gaining traction, that they had a chance to get this man in time, Connor turned and jogged back down the steep trail. They had him in their sights now. They were going to find him. There were only so many places he could be if he was hunting Jayne.

It was only at the bottom of the hill that Connor remembered, with a jolt, that he'd had another incoming call while he'd been getting all these developments in the case.

Quickly, he checked his phone, and felt his heart accelerate as he saw the call had been from Cami. In fact, she'd called twice.

She'd left a message after the second call.

"I think I know where Jayne has gone," she said, her voice tight with tension as he listened. "Connor, I'm going to start walking there. It's not on one of the routes you took. I can't wait."

Where was it? Where had Cami gone off to on her own?

He called her back, now feeling his heart racing with urgency. But Cami didn't pick up.

Connor clenched his fists, his fingers digging into his palms as he listened to the phone ring and ring and ring.

CHAPTER TWENTY NINE

Cami had figured it out. At least, she thought she had. She was pretty sure she now knew how he'd tracked—or was tracking—Jayne. And since it was evident that he had non-specialized IT knowledge, Cami now understood the other ingredient he'd used in this deadly mix.

Patience.

Because with all these intertwining trails and so many possible routes through the forest, it made sense that Jayne must be a creature of habit. For the killer to have gone in after her, he must have known where she'd be going. And that was because, like many people, Jayne would publish her exercise routes online.

Maybe she did the same route every time she taught at that school, Cami thought, now intent on exploring this idea. Or maybe she alternated, doing one route one day a week and the other the other day.

Whatever it was, she was now searching back in Jayne's archives, looking for a published route that she was now confident would be there. And, to her incredulous relief, she found one from a week ago. It wasn't in her main feed, which is why she hadn't seen it earlier. It was hidden away in an album entitled, "Vistas."

"I do love this walk! What a fabulous view it gives from the top of the hill! My post-coaching ritual!" Jayne had posted, exactly a week ago, with a photo of a forest hilltop surrounded by a sea of trees.

And alongside that happy comment, she'd posted a diagram of the route, just like many people did online when they wanted to show the world, or their followers, how far they'd walked.

Immediately, looking at it, Cami saw a big problem. This route hadn't been taken by Connor or his partner. They'd been discussing where to go, and they had picked the two trails that led in the most direct way back to Jayne's house.

This route was horrendously complicated. It wound its way through the trees, sometimes seeming to veer off the tracks entirely. There was no way anyone logical could have followed it, and that was because it wasn't a logical route, it was a customized route.

Devised through years of walking the woods, Jayne had chosen this because she liked it the best. Clearly, it met her demands for the distance, the elevation, and the view.

But it also satisfied someone else's needs. Because it was the ideal route for someone—armed with the basic technology Cami had seen—to monitor Jayne's movements.

And the killer was using that route.

He must have monitored her, Cami thought, feeling sick as she considered it. He'd watched Jayne posting her cheerful maps and photos, and he'd decided that it was his own route too. He'd tracked Jayne, and he'd memorized the route.

"Connor! He has to know," Cami gasped.

She called him immediately, punching in the number, waiting impatiently for the call to connect. But there was only a busy signal.

Cami sighed in frustration. Connor must be on another call. Connecting with the office, perhaps some kind of breakthrough had come in. But this couldn't wait. This was way too important.

And the problem was that from the direction they had gone, both Connor and the other team would be too far away.

She was closer.

She tried Connor again, but still no reply, and that meant she had to make a tough decision. *She could at least go,* Cami thought. She had to try to help. There was no way she could sit here now that she had discovered this bombshell. Every moment that passed could mean life or death for Jayne as she walked her beloved forest tracks.

Cami knew that she was going to have to head out alone. Hopefully, Connor would call her back as soon as he could, but in the meantime, she left a quick voicemail message saying she was heading out.

Taking a deep breath, Cami snapped open the locks and climbed out of the police car.

She felt exposed and scared. No technology, no IT knowhow, could help her now. She was feet on the ground, just like Connor, and she was realizing how vulnerable this left her.

She didn't have a gun. Not that a gun would be of any use to her. She'd be more likely to shoot herself in the foot than disable a criminal. Her only advantage was that Becker didn't know she was coming. And maybe, seeing she was just one woman on her own and not an obvious cop, that would give her a chance to get there in time, quickly and quietly, to rescue Jayne.

Her mouth dry with fear, Cami looked around her.

She was in the upper valley. It was a wide, open area, with a lake glinting in the distance. But she was going to have to go up an embankment and through a dense copse of trees.

Cami put her phone in her pocket. She put her laptop in the trunk of the car, took out the keys from the ignition, and locked it.

Then she set off up the hill, with the coordinates and route of Jayne's map fixed in her mind.

Even with the route in her head, Cami kept glancing around her, fearing to see a dark figure emerge from the shadows. The trees seemed to huddle around her, and she felt that sharp, prickling sensation of being watched.

Every step was taking her farther away from the safety of the police car. And farther away from the safety of Connor.

With every step she took, Becker seemed to be growing in her mind, from a cold-blooded killer to a monster.

A monster who could see her. A monster who could sense her. And he might be looking out for her, she realized. If he was in the woods, he could be waiting and watching, alert for any threat. Her heart thudded hard. This was a level of exposure she was very uncomfortable with.

Cami gritted her teeth and kept walking. If she wanted to save Jayne, she had no choice.

Suddenly, she froze. There was movement in the woods. Straight ahead. Cami's heart thudded hard.

Was that Jayne? Or the killer?

Her head was turning over, her eyes trying to make out what was there, as she kept moving forward, keeping her eyes trained on the spot of motion.

And then, as she watched, a deer emerged from the undergrowth, his head turning around to glance at her as he bounded up the hill, leaves and twigs crackling underfoot.

Cami exhaled and put her head in her hands.

"You idiot," she murmured. She turned back to her route, intending to keep walking, when she heard a sound so soft that, at first, she thought that she was imagining it.

It was the faint sound of a scream.

Cami froze, her eyes widening. She'd heard that sound. Had she imagined it? Was it something else? The cry of a bird, or maybe a big cat had made the sound?

It had come from ahead and sharply to the right. Which, as she remembered, was the way Jayne's route went.

As she listened, there was another loud, terrified scream. Cami's heart was pounding with fear, her body frozen to the spot. The scream had been from Jayne. It was real. No question about it. It had happened.

It hadn't been her imagination. That was her scared self-talking, trying to persuade her not to rush into danger. It had been a scream, and there was only one reason for it—the killer had caught up with Jayne.

And now, Cami had to catch up too. No other choice. And no time left, either.

Cami broke into a run, sprinting along the steep uphill track. She felt like she was choking on the lack of oxygen as she pushed herself to run faster, even though she feared it was already too late.

She dreaded being unable to get there in time to stop the killer. She had to move and move fast. Thinking fast, she also realized that she couldn't risk making any more noise. She needed to get closer without alerting him.

With that in mind, Cami stopped, quickly turning her phone to silent. That would mean she couldn't hear Connor's call. Thinking it might help, she messaged him her location. And then, she ran on again.

She reached the bend in the track, feeling breathless, cold with fear. There was nobody in sight. Nobody. Gasping, Cami looked around. He'd gone! Had he already killed her? Where was Jayne now?

Then, she remembered his modus operandi. Through the dense leaves, she could see the glimmer of the lake down a sharply sloping track.

Water.

Of course. He must be carrying her there to complete the drowning. And now, Cami had to get there, alone, to try to stop him.

CHAPTER THIRTY

Cami felt a sense of unreality as she powered down the steep hill, trying to move as silently as she could, slipping and sliding over the mud and leaves. She knew that she was on the right track. There, ahead, she could see that there was a dent in the mud, made by something heavy.

The boot of a killer carrying an unconscious victim, perhaps? That was the image she had in her mind. Was this Becker? Was she on his trail?

She had to be.

Cami powered on, launching herself downward, letting gravity do the work where her own strength was running short.

The mud was thick, wet, and heavy, pulling at her feet and slowing her down. She was making too much noise, she thought, and she worried that she was giving herself away. She forced herself to move more quietly while trying not to sacrifice speed.

She needed to catch up to them. It was the only thought in her mind. She had to find Jayne, and fast.

Her heart was pounding, her legs burning. She was running on pure adrenaline now. Her breath was short and quick, and she had the terrible sense that she was too late. And then, as she skidded to the bottom, she saw a splash of color, just a fleeting glimpse through the trees. A smudge of gray among the green. Was that her? Was he carrying her to the lake? She looked again, trying to read the terrain, trying to make sense of what she'd seen.

Slowing now, with the danger of her predicament weighing heavy on her, Cami stepped quietly through the trees. Ahead, through the dense brush, she could see the deep blue glimmer of the lake. This was where he was headed, she felt sure. The water must be drawing him like a magnet. For certain, it was the closest spot that he could use to kill.

Gasping in a breath, she saw him. Her hands clenched tightly as she caught sight of the rangy man. For the first time, she caught actual sight of this killer who had destroyed so many lives and who now had Jayne in his arms.

He was tall, with broad shoulders and a tousled shock of blond hair that looked as if it hadn't been cut or brushed for a long time. He wore ragged jeans and a brown plaid top.

He was strong. He was carrying Jayne with ease, as if he was just holding a doll. She was unconscious. Her limbs were limp, and she slumped in his grasp as he waded out into the lake. Cami wondered with a terrible clench of her heart whether she was even still alive. He could already have killed her. This could all be for nothing, but she had to try.

She couldn't see his face. His back was toward her. But he was already knee-deep in the water, and she knew that at any moment, he could drop Jayne, force her under, and she would die quickly.

He was muttering something.

"Granny," he said. The breeze carried his words back to her. "Granny, I thought it was you. It isn't, and now I must kill it. Maybe you'll come back then."

Hearing this deluded man speak to a long dead grandma chilled Cami's blood. Without a doubt, he was haunted by his memories of the crash and looking to find his family again. But he was finding them by killing people, and now Cami thought that the hunt for his family might be no more than a flimsy excuse to kill. That was what he was. A killer. Nothing more. Now that she'd seen him, she was sure of that. The scenarios in his mind were providing reasons for it, leading up to what he needed to do, and that was to murder.

Fear gripped Cami's heart and she took a long, deep breath, steeling herself for what she had to do. But she couldn't waste time in gathering her courage. He was moving and taking Jayne with him.

She had to move, and fast. What would she do?

She didn't have a plan. She needed a plan, but nothing came to mind.

But she had a weapon. Her gaze rested on a long wooden stick, lying by the side of the water. That must be his stick. He'd used it to attack Jayne, and he'd dropped it before heading out into the water.

It was something she could use. And she had to be quick, because to Cami's horror, she now saw that Jayne was starting to wake up. Her limbs were flailing weakly. He hadn't hit her hard enough. At least she was alive for the moment, but now there was no time left at all. He was going to drown her for sure.

Right now, she was being cradled against his chest. Just inches away from the cold water.

Without thinking too much more about it, Cami raced forward. She grabbed the stick and then, knowing that he'd hear her for sure as soon as her feet hit the water, she jumped into the lake and ran toward him with all the speed she could manage.

The water was a cold shock on her legs. Sure enough, the splash alerted him, and he twisted around, staggering a little under the weight of the now struggling woman in his arms.

Yelling at the top of her voice, more because she was scared herself than because she hoped to scare him, Cami rushed him with the stick held high.

He lifted an arm to defend himself, instinctively. And Jayne's legs slipped out of his grasp. Cami felt a wash of relief that she was, at least, free of him. She landed clumsily, but on her feet, in the water, looking dizzy and sick, immediately stumbling down to her knees. But she was conscious, she was breathing, and the water was shallow enough that her head was above it. Better still, she was now out of his way.

But now, all his focus was on Cami. She was trapped in his gaze, face to face with a furious, narrow-eyed adversary.

And Cami attacked, bringing the stick down with all her force, not caring where she managed to hit this terrible, psychopathic man, but only caring that she managed to hit him.

The first blow didn't land well at all. He saw her attack coming and brought his arm up to block it, managing to deflect it to the side, so it hit him in the shoulder. He yelled in rage. The anger in his tone felt like a physical force.

But she couldn't stop, couldn't give up. Jayne was still struggling in the shallows, still trying to come around from the blow he must have given her. Cami had to stay in this fight, or he would go for Jayne again, and this time, she didn't doubt that he'd get her.

Cami brought the stick down again, aiming for his head this time. She needed to knock him out. Otherwise, she was sure that she would be all out of chances, and she didn't want to think about what his retaliation would be like.

She gritted her teeth, putting all her force into it. But he ducked, twisting desperately aside, and to her dismay, her blow missed. And then, before she had a chance to regroup, he was on her.

He grabbed her by the shoulders, his face cold and angry. His grasp was like steel. His strength was immense.

"You're going to drown too," he said, hissing out the words. "You shouldn't have followed me, little girl."

And with that, he shoved her under the water.

CHAPTER THIRTY ONE

Cami felt terror like she'd never felt before. The water was shockingly cold, and she hadn't had a chance to take a breath before his attack. Already, her lungs were screaming for air. She tried to fight him off, but his hands were like iron. He was so much stronger than her.

She had to fight, to do something. This water wasn't deep, Perhaps she could push off from the bottom. Perhaps she could kick out, knock him off balance.

Cami decided, then and there, that she was not going to give up. She was not going to allow him to drown her in thigh-deep water but was going to fight with everything she had for as long as she could.

She grabbed blindly at his legs, tugging at the ripped denim, hoping she could somehow gain an advantage this way. Her lungs were threatening to explode now. She was having to fight with everything she had to stop herself from gasping in a breath of what would not be the air her body was begging for, but a cold flood of water.

Cami kicked out with all her might, wanting to land a blow that would at least make him let go long enough for her to get a breath.

But he was expecting her to do that, and he held her tightly, preventing her from getting a blow in. Still he held her under. With his hand like a steel pincer on her shoulder, he forced her down. She couldn't get a foothold on the muddy bottom. His fingers were so tight on her shoulders that she could hardly move.

She knew, with a terrible certainty, that this was the end. She was going to die. She had failed. But she was not giving up, not until she couldn't struggle anymore.

Cami kicked again and her foot landed hard against something. She had the briefest of moments to register the fact that she'd kicked his knee and then she felt him stagger. She felt his hands loosen. Her Doc Marten, with its hard sole and steel toecap, had done the job. It had hurt him enough to derail his murderous mission. With all her strength, Cami writhed away, stamping down on the uneven, slippery surface. And she did it. She broke the surface, choking and gasping for air. She was still half blinded by the muddy water. Her eyes were stinging. The lake and the landscape were half blurred. She had to get out before he grabbed her again.

Turning away, she plunged toward the shore, seeing that Jayne had managed to fight her way into the shallows and was crawling determinedly out of the lake.

But behind her, she heard an angry shout and a surge of water as he launched himself in pursuit, and she knew with a thrill of terror that the danger was not over yet. He could grab her at any moment and then, if he drowned her, Jayne was far too weak and disoriented still to escape. She'd made her way to the edge of the water, but that was about all she could do.

Now, she knew that at any moment she would feel his hands grabbing her back, and he would force her down, crushing her head into the lake's shallow, muddy bottom, finishing the kills that he was now hell bent on committing.

There was no saving her now, Cami knew. She'd been lucky once and could not be so lucky again, but still, she was not going to give up. She was going to keep running, right up until the moment where he grabbed her and didn't let go.

And then she saw another figure, ahead of her, in her blurred vision. Through streaming eyes she saw it. Racing from the edge of the woods to the lake. His posture looked familiar, his hand stretched out ahead of him. And she heard the voice she recognized, sharp and urgent.

Connor's voice.

"Cami, down! Get down!"

She knew instantly what that meant, what he was going to do, and what she had to do to save herself.

Cami dove down, hitting the water, gasping in another breath as she flattened herself in the muddy shallows.

And then a crack split the air, searing her ears.

Behind her, there was a tumbling splash. And then, silence.

Cami scrambled up out of the water. She stumbled to the shore's edge, heading straight over to Jayne, helping her out of the water.

Only then did she dare look back to where Connor was rushing into the lake, his gun still drawn.

He was staring down into the shallows, but Cami realized with a feeling of utter relief that his bullet had found its mark. His shot had been accurate. And now, in the waters of the lake, Becker himself was lifeless, just as his victims had been.

Cami gasped in a sob, holding tightly to Jayne's hand as they stared at the body in the lake, while Connor bent down and checked the man's pulse. Then, straight away, he turned to Cami and Jayne, urgency in his face.

"Are you okay?" he asked, striding toward them, already on the phone. "Get the ambulance," he barked to whomever answered. "I'll send coordinates now."

"Are you alright?" Cami asked Jayne. She was pretty, with a kind face, though mud streaked. A graze on her temple showed where Becker had hit her—though not hard enough. She was looking totally confused, but there was a little color back in her face now.

"I'm okay. I think I was attacked. I can't remember what happened exactly." She stared at the lake, frowning. "This feels like a dream, but it can't be? Did the FBI really race here and shoot him?"

"Just in time, ma'am," Connor said, his voice firm. "The ambulance is on the way now, but for the moment, just sit down and rest. You don't want to risk moving after a head injury, until you've been checked out." He turned to Cami. "And you, Cami? I saw you in the lake as I was running through the trees. You fought him off!" There was a tone of admiration in his voice she'd never heard before.

"I know. I didn't think I could, but I had to try. I'm just glad you got here."

"I picked up your message. Saw the coordinates," Connor said.

"My phone!" Cami grabbed at her jacket pocket. It had been underwater for some time. As quickly as she could, she turned it off. If that water got into the circuit board, it would fry the entire system. She took it apart, removing the battery, shaking out the water.

"It might be okay if I leave it overnight and pack it in rice or silica gel," she said. There was information on it she needed. She'd done a recent backup, but not everything had synced online or to her laptop. Hopefully the other data on there could be saved.

"I hope your phone will be fine, Cami," Connor said, with sympathy in his tone. "And if it isn't, then since it was damaged in the course of fighting crime, you can get a new one. On us. The FBI will buy it for you to replace yours."

"Thanks," she said, feeling pleased that they would spring for a new phone if it was needed.

"You did an exceptional job there. These were highly dangerous circumstances, and you were in a combat situation. I've known trained agents who wouldn't have managed to keep fighting and do what you did out there. I know Fraser is going to be proud of what you've done. Jacenta too."

He cast another concerned glance at Jayne, but Cami thought she was looking stronger now and starting to rally. And in the distance, she heard the wail of sirens. The ambulance was on the way.

"I never thought I'd be able to do such a thing. I guess I've learned a lot from you." They exchanged a quick grin at that, but Cami's expression quickly faded as she glanced again at the lake.

She'd been in so much danger. And in the end, this brutal, damaged man had died, claimed by the waters of a lake.

His violent life was over. And thanks to their effort and risk, his final victim was still alive.

EPILOGUE

Cami didn't want to do this. In fact, she'd never thought she would be able to bring herself to do it.

But it was the only way that she was going to be able to piece together the puzzle surrounding Jenna and to find out if anything really was missing from the case file.

She wasn't good at what she was planning to do. She didn't know if she had what it took at all, or even where to start. Definitely, she'd gone into IT because the logic and processes appealed to her. The chaos inherent in human relationships? Not so much.

But she couldn't put this off forever, and so, she picked up the phone.

She dialed her father's number. This was still saved on her contacts list as "Home," even though it had been years since she'd thought of it that way. Had that charmless little house, with its leaky roof and its undesirable location near the factories, ever really been a home to anyone? That was something she doubted.

It wasn't home. Even so, for now, maybe it could give her answers. She'd waited until six-thirty p.m., knowing he'd be home by then, not wanting to waste all the courage she'd summoned, only to have him not pick up.

Nerves twisted inside her as she heard the phone ring. And then, his voice harsh, her father answered.

"Lark speaking."

"Dad. It's Cami."

There was a surprised silence. Then, her father spoke again, but the harshness was still in his voice. What had she thought? That he'd be overjoyed to hear his estranged daughter, after everything that had happened between them?

The fights. The rebellion. The way Cami had resisted his natural tendency to dominate their home. The way she and her sister had secretly supported each other, eroding his control, and resisting his punishments.

"Cami?" he said. "Why are you calling?"

Cami was sure that at six-thirty, her silent mother would already be in the kitchen preparing supper. And she was sure that upon hearing her daughter's name, her head would jerk up, her expression both worried and hopeful. She'd be trying to pick up what she could from the conversation, Cami knew, remembering her mother's whispered words of support that had come far too seldom. She'd be too scared to come through and listen, or to ask her father why Cami had called.

But she'd be listening. For sure. Cami knew what her mother's face would look like. She could picture it now.

"I wanted to talk to you," Cami said.

"About what?" he asked.

Time to unleash what Cami suspected would be a bombshell.

"I wanted to know about Jenna," Cami said. "I wanted to know what happened to her. Dad, I need to understand why the FBI got nowhere with that case."

She heard her father exhale. It sounded like he'd actually been holding his breath.

"There's nothing to say," he said, his voice flat.

"There must be!" Cami argued. "I know there must have been more to the case. What happened? Why did it get nowhere?"

"None of your business," he said in a tone that was final.

"What happened to her?" Cami asked again. "Why did you abandon her?"

"Cami," her father said, his voice tight. "I don't want to talk about this."

"You have to talk about it," Cami said, angry now, her voice rising. "It's important. It's my life. It's my sister's life. It's all of our lives."

"I don't know what you mean," her father said, his words clipped. His tone was impatient now, as if Cami was making a nuisance of herself.

"You know what I mean," Cami said. "I've been doing some research."

"You've been snooping around?" her father asked. "Playing detective?" His tone was heavily sarcastic. There was no way she was going to tell him that she'd been working for the FBI. Now was not the time for that. It would complicate the situation. It would not endear him to her at all.

"It's more like being a researcher. I suspect there was information on the case that never made it into the file. I'd like to know if that's true.

Because if it is, aren't you angry? As a policeman yourself, didn't you want things to be done right?"

Her father was silent. Was it possible that the logical argument had convinced him? Was he going to finally tell her what she knew was being left unsaid?

He sighed heavily. "Cami, no," he said. "I'm not ready to do that. And you need to stop asking. If you know what is good for you."

There was a pause as if he was about to say something else. And then there was a click.

He'd disconnected the call. Cami drew in a sharp, affronted, dismayed breath. He'd just cut her off! How was she ever going to find out the truth?

She stood up from her seat in her small student room and paced back and forth, wondering what her next move should be. The room was big enough for four paces, wall to wall. Angrily, feeling like a caged lion, she strode the distance.

And then, just as she was still taking in that her father had so rudely told her no, her phone rang.

It was “Home.” Had he reconsidered?

Hope flaring, Cami answered the call. But to her astonishment, she found herself speaking to her mother, her voice a semi whisper.

"Cami!"

"Mom?"

"Your dad's gone out. I think he was angry after the call."

"He has?" Cami asked warily. “Why are you calling me, then?”

Her mother hesitated. "Listen, don't tell him I called. I . . . I overheard the conversation. And what you were asking."

"Do you know more?" Cami said. Of course her mother knew more. As silent and submissive as she might be, but she had listened at the right times, Cami was sure.

"Yes. I don't know everything. But I know that Jenna was somehow involved with an older man. I don't think it was romantic. I think it was something else—at first, anyway. He was trouble. I knew it immediately. I wanted them to investigate him but they never did, and the case seemed to somehow disappear after that."

The words rushed out of her mother as if she'd held them in for a long time.

Cami couldn't believe it. She felt as if she'd been physically slapped in the face by this knowledge. There had been someone who'd withheld evidence. Jenna had gotten caught up in something, but what, Cami had no idea.

"Who is this man?" Cami asked.

"I heard his name once."

"What is it?"

"Liam. Liam Treverton." Her mother hesitated. "Your dad's coming back. I must go."

She cut the call, leaving Cami feeling paralyzed by disbelief.

Jenna had been involved with Liam Treverton before she went missing and the case had been sabotaged.

Liam Treverton was the FBI agent who'd handled the missing persons case and who'd since been dismissed from the Bureau in disgrace.

Staring down at his name, Cami felt a cold rage build inside her. She was going to pursue this, by whatever means it took, and no matter the risk to herself. And she knew what her next move would be.

JUST FORGET
(A Cami Lark Mystery—Book 4)

With her tattoos and piercings, MIT tech genius Cami Lark is rebellious and anti-authoritarian—and finds herself in deep trouble when she hacks the FBI. Faced with the choice of prison or aiding the BAU hunt down serial killers, Cami reluctantly partners. But as victims turn up in a chillingly normal setting, Cami realizes that, unless she cracks the tech riddle, more will turn up soon. Can Cami handle the pressure?

"A masterpiece of thriller and mystery."
—Books and Movie Reviews, Roberto Mattos (re Once Gone)

JUST FORGET (A Cami Lark FBI Suspense Thriller—Book 4) is the fourth novel in a new series by #1 bestseller and USA Today bestselling author Blake Pierce, whose bestseller Once Gone (a free download) has received over 7,000 five star ratings and reviews.

A page-turning and harrowing crime thriller featuring a brilliant and tortured FBI agent, the CAMI LARK series is a riveting mystery, packed with non-stop action, suspense, twists and turns, revelations, and driven by a breakneck pace that will keep you flipping pages late into the night. Fans of Rachel Caine, Teresa Driscoll and Robert Dugoni are sure to fall in love.

Future books in the series are also now available.

"An edge of your seat thriller in a new series that keeps you turning pages! ...So many twists, turns and red herrings… I can't wait to see what happens next."
—Reader review (Her Last Wish)

"A strong, complex story about two FBI agents trying to stop a serial killer. If you want an author to capture your attention and have you guessing, yet trying to put the pieces together, Pierce is your author!"
—Reader review (Her Last Wish)

"A typical Blake Pierce twisting, turning, roller coaster ride suspense thriller. Will have you turning the pages to the last sentence of the last chapter!!!"

—Reader review (City of Prey)

"Right from the start we have an unusual protagonist that I haven't seen done in this genre before. The action is nonstop… A very atmospheric novel that will keep you turning pages well into the wee hours."

—Reader review (City of Prey)

"Everything that I look for in a book… a great plot, interesting characters, and grabs your interest right away. The book moves along at a breakneck pace and stays that way until the end. Now on go I to book two!"

—Reader review (Girl, Alone)

Blake Pierce

Blake Pierce is the USA Today bestselling author of the RILEY PAGE mystery series, which includes seventeen books. Blake Pierce is also the author of the MACKENZIE WHITE mystery series, comprising fourteen books; of the AVERY BLACK mystery series, comprising six books; of the KERI LOCKE mystery series, comprising five books; of the MAKING OF RILEY PAIGE mystery series, comprising six books; of the KATE WISE mystery series, comprising seven books; of the CHLOE FINE psychological suspense mystery, comprising six books; of the JESSIE HUNT psychological suspense thriller series, comprising twenty six books; of the AU PAIR psychological suspense thriller series, comprising three books; of the ZOE PRIME mystery series, comprising six books; of the ADELE SHARP mystery series, comprising sixteen books, of the EUROPEAN VOYAGE cozy mystery series, comprising six books; of the LAURA FROST FBI suspense thriller, comprising eleven books; of the ELLA DARK FBI suspense thriller, comprising fourteen books (and counting); of the A YEAR IN EUROPE cozy mystery series, comprising nine books, of the AVA GOLD mystery series, comprising six books (and counting); of the RACHEL GIFT mystery series, comprising ten books (and counting); of the VALERIE LAW mystery series, comprising nine books (and counting); of the PAIGE KING mystery series, comprising eight books (and counting); of the MAY MOORE mystery series, comprising eleven books (and counting); the CORA SHIELDS mystery series, comprising five books (and counting); of the NICKY LYONS mystery series, comprising seven books (and counting), of the CAMI LARK mystery series, comprising five books (and counting), and of the new AMBER YOUNG mystery series, comprising five books (and counting).

An avid reader and lifelong fan of the mystery and thriller genres, Blake loves to hear from you, so please feel free to visit www.blakepierceauthor.com to learn more and stay in touch.

BOOKS BY BLAKE PIERCE

AMBER YOUNG MYSTERY SERIES
ABSENT PITY (Book #1)
ABSENT REMORSE (Book #2)
ABSENT FEELING (Book #3)
ABSENT MERCY (Book #4)
ABSENT REASON (Book #5)

CAMI LARK MYSTERY SERIES
JUST ME (Book #1)
JUST OUTSIDE (Book #2)
JUST RIGHT (Book #3)
JUST FORGET (Book #4)
JUST ONCE (Book #5)

NICKY LYONS MYSTERY SERIES
ALL MINE (Book #1)
ALL HIS (Book #2)
ALL HE SEES (Book #3)
ALL ALONE (Book #4)
ALL FOR ONE (Book #5)
ALL HE TAKES (Book #6)
ALL FOR ME (Book #7)

CORA SHIELDS MYSTERY SERIES
UNDONE (Book #1)
UNWANTED (Book #2)
UNHINGED (Book #3)
UNSAID (Book #4)
UNGLUED (Book #5)

MAY MOORE SUSPENSE THRILLER
NEVER RUN (Book #1)
NEVER TELL (Book #2)
NEVER LIVE (Book #3)
NEVER HIDE (Book #4)

NEVER FORGIVE (Book #5)
NEVER AGAIN (Book #6)
NEVER LOOK BACK (Book #7)
NEVER FORGET (Book #8)
NEVER LET GO (Book #9)
NEVER PRETEND (Book #10)
NEVER HESITATE (Book #11)

PAIGE KING MYSTERY SERIES
THE GIRL HE PINED (Book #1)
THE GIRL HE CHOSE (Book #2)
THE GIRL HE TOOK (Book #3)
THE GIRL HE WISHED (Book #4)
THE GIRL HE CROWNED (Book #5)
THE GIRL HE WATCHED (Book #6)
THE GIRL HE WANTED (Book #7)
THE GIRL HE CLAIMED (Book #8)

VALERIE LAW MYSTERY SERIES
NO MERCY (Book #1)
NO PITY (Book #2)
NO FEAR (Book #3)
NO SLEEP (Book #4)
NO QUARTER (Book #5)
NO CHANCE (Book #6)
NO REFUGE (Book #7)
NO GRACE (Book #8)
NO ESCAPE (Book #9)

RACHEL GIFT MYSTERY SERIES
HER LAST WISH (Book #1)
HER LAST CHANCE (Book #2)
HER LAST HOPE (Book #3)
HER LAST FEAR (Book #4)
HER LAST CHOICE (Book #5)
HER LAST BREATH (Book #6)
HER LAST MISTAKE (Book #7)
HER LAST DESIRE (Book #8)
HER LAST REGRET (Book #9)
HER LAST HOUR (Book #10)

AVA GOLD MYSTERY SERIES
CITY OF PREY (Book #1)
CITY OF FEAR (Book #2)
CITY OF BONES (Book #3)
CITY OF GHOSTS (Book #4)
CITY OF DEATH (Book #5)
CITY OF VICE (Book #6)

A YEAR IN EUROPE
A MURDER IN PARIS (Book #1)
DEATH IN FLORENCE (Book #2)
VENGEANCE IN VIENNA (Book #3)
A FATALITY IN SPAIN (Book #4)

ELLA DARK FBI SUSPENSE THRILLER
GIRL, ALONE (Book #1)
GIRL, TAKEN (Book #2)
GIRL, HUNTED (Book #3)
GIRL, SILENCED (Book #4)
GIRL, VANISHED (Book 5)
GIRL ERASED (Book #6)
GIRL, FORSAKEN (Book #7)
GIRL, TRAPPED (Book #8)
GIRL, EXPENDABLE (Book #9)
GIRL, ESCAPED (Book #10)
GIRL, HIS (Book #11)
GIRL, LURED (Book #12)
GIRL, MISSING (Book #13)
GIRL, UNKNOWN (Book #14)

LAURA FROST FBI SUSPENSE THRILLER
ALREADY GONE (Book #1)
ALREADY SEEN (Book #2)
ALREADY TRAPPED (Book #3)
ALREADY MISSING (Book #4)
ALREADY DEAD (Book #5)
ALREADY TAKEN (Book #6)
ALREADY CHOSEN (Book #7)
ALREADY LOST (Book #8)

ALREADY HIS (Book #9)
ALREADY LURED (Book #10)
ALREADY COLD (Book #11)

EUROPEAN VOYAGE COZY MYSTERY SERIES
MURDER (AND BAKLAVA) (Book #1)
DEATH (AND APPLE STRUDEL) (Book #2)
CRIME (AND LAGER) (Book #3)
MISFORTUNE (AND GOUDA) (Book #4)
CALAMITY (AND A DANISH) (Book #5)
MAYHEM (AND HERRING) (Book #6)

ADELE SHARP MYSTERY SERIES
LEFT TO DIE (Book #1)
LEFT TO RUN (Book #2)
LEFT TO HIDE (Book #3)
LEFT TO KILL (Book #4)
LEFT TO MURDER (Book #5)
LEFT TO ENVY (Book #6)
LEFT TO LAPSE (Book #7)
LEFT TO VANISH (Book #8)
LEFT TO HUNT (Book #9)
LEFT TO FEAR (Book #10)
LEFT TO PREY (Book #11)
LEFT TO LURE (Book #12)
LEFT TO CRAVE (Book #13)
LEFT TO LOATHE (Book #14)
LEFT TO HARM (Book #15)
LEFT TO RUIN (Book #16)

THE AU PAIR SERIES
ALMOST GONE (Book#1)
ALMOST LOST (Book #2)
ALMOST DEAD (Book #3)

ZOE PRIME MYSTERY SERIES
FACE OF DEATH (Book#1)
FACE OF MURDER (Book #2)
FACE OF FEAR (Book #3)
FACE OF MADNESS (Book #4)

FACE OF FURY (Book #5)
FACE OF DARKNESS (Book #6)

A JESSIE HUNT PSYCHOLOGICAL SUSPENSE SERIES
THE PERFECT WIFE (Book #1)
THE PERFECT BLOCK (Book #2)
THE PERFECT HOUSE (Book #3)
THE PERFECT SMILE (Book #4)
THE PERFECT LIE (Book #5)
THE PERFECT LOOK (Book #6)
THE PERFECT AFFAIR (Book #7)
THE PERFECT ALIBI (Book #8)
THE PERFECT NEIGHBOR (Book #9)
THE PERFECT DISGUISE (Book #10)
THE PERFECT SECRET (Book #11)
THE PERFECT FAÇADE (Book #12)
THE PERFECT IMPRESSION (Book #13)
THE PERFECT DECEIT (Book #14)
THE PERFECT MISTRESS (Book #15)
THE PERFECT IMAGE (Book #16)
THE PERFECT VEIL (Book #17)
THE PERFECT INDISCRETION (Book #18)
THE PERFECT RUMOR (Book #19)
THE PERFECT COUPLE (Book #20)
THE PERFECT MURDER (Book #21)
THE PERFECT HUSBAND (Book #22)
THE PERFECT SCANDAL (Book #23)
THE PERFECT MASK (Book #24)
THE PERFECT RUSE (Book #25)
THE PERFECT VENEER (Book #26)

CHLOE FINE PSYCHOLOGICAL SUSPENSE SERIES
NEXT DOOR (Book #1)
A NEIGHBOR'S LIE (Book #2)
CUL DE SAC (Book #3)
SILENT NEIGHBOR (Book #4)
HOMECOMING (Book #5)
TINTED WINDOWS (Book #6)

KATE WISE MYSTERY SERIES

IF SHE KNEW (Book #1)
IF SHE SAW (Book #2)
IF SHE RAN (Book #3)
IF SHE HID (Book #4)
IF SHE FLED (Book #5)
IF SHE FEARED (Book #6)
IF SHE HEARD (Book #7)

THE MAKING OF RILEY PAIGE SERIES
WATCHING (Book #1)
WAITING (Book #2)
LURING (Book #3)
TAKING (Book #4)
STALKING (Book #5)
KILLING (Book #6)

RILEY PAIGE MYSTERY SERIES
ONCE GONE (Book #1)
ONCE TAKEN (Book #2)
ONCE CRAVED (Book #3)
ONCE LURED (Book #4)
ONCE HUNTED (Book #5)
ONCE PINED (Book #6)
ONCE FORSAKEN (Book #7)
ONCE COLD (Book #8)
ONCE STALKED (Book #9)
ONCE LOST (Book #10)
ONCE BURIED (Book #11)
ONCE BOUND (Book #12)
ONCE TRAPPED (Book #13)
ONCE DORMANT (Book #14)
ONCE SHUNNED (Book #15)
ONCE MISSED (Book #16)
ONCE CHOSEN (Book #17)

MACKENZIE WHITE MYSTERY SERIES
BEFORE HE KILLS (Book #1)
BEFORE HE SEES (Book #2)
BEFORE HE COVETS (Book #3)
BEFORE HE TAKES (Book #4)

BEFORE HE NEEDS (Book #5)
BEFORE HE FEELS (Book #6)
BEFORE HE SINS (Book #7)
BEFORE HE HUNTS (Book #8)
BEFORE HE PREYS (Book #9)
BEFORE HE LONGS (Book #10)
BEFORE HE LAPSES (Book #11)
BEFORE HE ENVIES (Book #12)
BEFORE HE STALKS (Book #13)
BEFORE HE HARMS (Book #14)

AVERY BLACK MYSTERY SERIES
CAUSE TO KILL (Book #1)
CAUSE TO RUN (Book #2)
CAUSE TO HIDE (Book #3)
CAUSE TO FEAR (Book #4)
CAUSE TO SAVE (Book #5)
CAUSE TO DREAD (Book #6)

KERI LOCKE MYSTERY SERIES
A TRACE OF DEATH (Book #1)
A TRACE OF MURDER (Book #2)
A TRACE OF VICE (Book #3)
A TRACE OF CRIME (Book #4)
A TRACE OF HOPE (Book #5)

Made in United States
Orlando, FL
11 July 2023

34965053R10098